The Precious Quartet

Selected Tales from Bên Kia Bến Đỗ

by

Vinh Q. Tang

Cover picture reproduced from a drawing generously
gifted by Dr. Truong Vo-Van.

Nghĩa Lan Nhân

Acknowledgment

The translation of selected contents from a Vietnamese book, 'Bên Kia Bến Đỗ,' by the same author, has been facilitated with significant assistance from Chat GPT.

Vinh Quyen Tang
Ottawa, 01-01-2024

Contents

1. The Fate of a Woman 6

2. Silent Pain 18

3. The Quartet of Colette 24

4. Tomb-Sweeping Day 29

5. The Surrogate Mother 37

6. Facing the Devil 41

7. The Awaited Dawn 51

8. Nurse Thanh 59

9. A Magical Event 65

10. Familial Duty 82

11. A Military Spouse 91

12. The Quartet Reunion 98

Notes 121

Author 122

1. The Fate of a Woman

Beneath the scorching Saigon sun, just a fortnight before Japanese forces would sweep away the colonial French regime in the throes of World War II, Mr. Tư, a formidable police officer often seen with a tightly clenched brown pipe between his lips, stood as a silent witness. In the midst of Saigon's typically bustling streets, now eerily emptied of their usual inhabitants, Japanese soldiers engaged in rigorous daily training.

Their resolute expressions and unwavering grip on rifles adorned with bayonets conveyed a palpable determination, seemingly unaffected by the presence of the current French authorities in Vietnam. In that moment, Mr. Tư foresaw the nation teetering on the brink of a transformative shift in occupying power.

"Sooner or later, this police station is destined to fall into the hands of the Japanese army," Mr. Tư whispered to himself, alluding to the police station in the Second District of Saigon where he dutifully served. Swiftly, he gathered Mrs. Tư and his two daughters, Nhàn and Thanh (You can call them Nan and Thanne), ushering them to the bus terminal bound for his hometown nestled in the Mekong Delta region of Cai Lậy, seeking refuge from the impending turmoil.

Six months later, in the serenity of a quiet field on a tranquil evening, the sun began its descent, casting shadows on the swaying bamboo. A handful of golden rays conspired with Thanh to extend the fleeting moment of daydreaming for a young urban girl compelled to escape the war-ravaged city and seek solace in her ancestral homeland.

Beside the fragrant vegetable patch near the ridge of white mangrove trees, Thanh perched on a plank at the riverbank's edge, engrossed in the task of washing dishes. Her eyes remained fixed on the water in the basin before her. A flood of memories inundated her heart, centered around Tâm, the man who inhabited her dreams. With her long, slender arm swaying gracefully in front of her knees, she rocked the final cup of water in the basin, repeatedly scooping and pouring, as if endeavoring to rejuvenate her recollections and fill her mind to overflowing.

From the horizon, the gentle breeze carried the fragrance of alluvial soil across the expansive rice fields. Drifting down the Nine Dragons River, once a guiding force for generations of pioneers cultivating and settling in the heartland of the South, were clusters of water hyacinths. A few lingering purple flowers, remnants of the dawn, swayed and bobbed, tracing an uncertain path on the journey that lay ahead.

"Thanh, why have you been outside for so long? Hurry in and help your sister with her bath," Mrs. Tư's voice called out from inside the house, pulling Thanh back to reality. She was Thanh's stepmother, a fact known to few outsiders, yet she embraced her role with wholehearted love and care for her stepchildren as if they were her own. Six years ago, tragedy struck when Thanh's birth mother met her untimely end in an accident that left an enduring scar on everyone's hearts.

In what initially appeared as a trivial incident, a minor cut on her thumb while scaling a fish for a family meal resulted in unforeseen consequences. Despite the superficial nature of the wound, her hand swelled the following day, and despite attempting various traditional remedies, none could alleviate her condition. Within two weeks, she succumbed to the illness, leaving three orphaned children in her wake. Thanh, the youngest, and Bình, the eldest son who had already joined the resistance against the French, had already left home. Thanh's elder sister, Nhàn, two years her senior, unfortunately contracted polio in childhood, making mobility difficult. Consequently, Thanh assumed the responsibility of assisting her stepmother in caring for Nhàn.

Before stepping inside the house, Thanh hesitated, lingering by the row of tamaru trees. She took a moment to quietly absorb the surroundings, realizing that these serene moments would soon be replaced by the bustling city life awaiting her in the coming days. As her gaze extended into the distance, past the lush green grove of water coconut palms lining the riverbank, the sight of the tall white mangrove atop a mound, bathed in the golden hues of the setting sun, invoked memories of Tâm.

In the days preceding her evacuation from the city, Thanh would approach the window each night, stealing glances through the thin curtain to locate the bright yellow glow in the hushed night. It emanated from the lone street lamp at the end of the soldier's barracks next to the Xây-nho police station. Her heart would race with anticipation, yearning to catch a glimpse of a silhouette named Tâm, seated immobile beneath the light, eyes fixed on the book in hand.

Little did Thanh know that, at that time, Tâm wasn't engrossed in his usual studies but was dedicated to learning Japanese. In the wake of the world-changing events of World War II, while in Europe, Germany was displacing the French and establishing puppet governments sympathetic to its cause, in Asia, Japan was extending its occupation to various territories, including many parts of Vietnam. With the imminent shift in rulership from French to Japanese in Vietnam, many seized the opportunity to learn Japanese, harboring dreams of a better life, aspiring to become interpreters or secretaries for the Japanese forces, much like the previous generations who had worked under French rule.

In any colonial regime, possessing knowledge of the language spoken by the ruling power and demonstrating a willingness to cooperate with foreign authorities often brought advantages. However, Tâm appeared to be on a distinct mission aligned with a revolutionary faction, setting him apart from those who sought personal gains.

The image of Tâm sitting serenely, engrossed in a book by the roadside, remained a steadfast refuge for Thanh. Despite the tumultuous world swirling around them, Tâm's calm demeanor served as a reassuring anchor. It bestowed upon Thanh a rare tranquility, akin to a miraculous elixir that cast a serene spell over her each night. The nocturnal darkness concealed the harrowing truths of the day - mysteries that Thanh, at her tender age, hadn't comprehended fully but intuited through the eyes of adults, the whispered conversations, and the veiled remarks of her parents and neighbors. These concealed truths encompassed secret societies, revolutions, assassinations, torture, elimination, and all forms of agony and gruesome demise, camouflaged beneath the veneer of sanctity or demonic deception.

"Thanh, why haven't you come home yet?" Mrs. Tư's voice urged Thanh to take Nhàn to the river for a bath, a daily duty for Thanh since the two sisters found refuge in the countryside. Thanh quickly closed the pages of memories, hurried home along the quiet, flowing river.

Mrs. Tư brought a chair outside, settling beside the loom on the front porch to savor the afternoon breeze. Through the open gate nestled between two bamboo rows, the silhouette of Mrs. Sáu emerged, slightly stooped as she made her way inside.

Mrs. Sáu, a resident of Rạch Dừa village, was renowned for her expertise in matchmaking. To find her, one simply needed to visit the bustling Rạch Dừa market, open daily on the bank of the Twin River, starting before the rooster's first crow. Despite its village setting, the market teemed with activity as people from nearby villages gathered for their daily shopping. Some came to buy and sell goods, but Mrs. Sáu's purpose was unique - she frequented the market to eavesdrop, keenly listening for information about households that had recently welcomed newborn sons or daughters.

Upon identifying mothers with single sons or daughters, Mrs. Sáu approached them with warmth, showering them with attention and staying close as they navigated from the fabric section on the upper market down to the fish stalls on the lower market by the riverbank.

This routine proved fruitful when, just one day after Mrs. Tư and her family relocated to the neighboring Phú Quý village, the news reached Mrs. Sáu's ears. She promptly began establishing acquaintance with Mrs. Tư outside the market. Today presented Mrs. Sáu with the opportunity to "see the joints and bones" of Mrs. Tư's daughter, a phrase in the language of matchmakers referring to the assessment of whether the daughter is suitable for the son of another family, and, perhaps more crucially, whether the potential bride is acceptable in the eyes of the future mother-in-law.

As Mrs. Sáu entered the courtyard, she respectfully bowed to greet Mrs. Tư, her mouth filled with a wad of chewed tobacco that protruded from the corner. With cheerful familiarity, she addressed Mrs. Tư as if they had known each other for a long time:

"Dear Mrs. Tư, how are you? It's been a while since I've seen you out at the market."

"Thank you, Sister Sáu. I am fine. Which wind blew you here today?"

"Oh, I won't hide it from you, Mrs. Tư. Today, I had the chance to visit Mr. and Mrs. Hộ (a title reserved for a very rich land owner in the countryside) at the upper village and decided to stop by to bring you and the two girls some fresh star apple fruit from my garden. You know, a few years ago, following the advice of our neighbors, my husband tried to plant a star apple fruit tree in front of our house. Surprisingly, it bore fruit for two seasons already. Let me tell you, it may not bear a lot, but the good thing is that each fruit is worth the effort. You know, it's so … so sweet. That's why yesterday he picked a few ripe ones to bring over here for you and the two girls to try."

Without completing her sentence, Mrs. Sáu requested permission to go straight to the back of the house to fetch a plate for displaying the fresh fruits on the table. In reality, this was just an excuse for her to meet Thanh and take the opportunity to observe the interior of the house, gauging its level of wealth or poverty. She paid particular attention to the kitchen, as her experience taught her that a tidy and organized kitchen reflected a woman's proficiency in housekeeping and household affairs. "A good mother raises a good child," she often remarked.

Unable to stand up in time to stop Mrs. Sáu, Mrs. Tư sat back and said, "Really! Sorry to have bothered you so much. You had gone through the trouble of bringing the fruits here, and now..."

Mrs. Tư meant to say "... Now you are even serving us," but she was interrupted by Mrs. Sáu's voice from the back of the house: "Wonder if Miss Thanh is at home, Mrs. Tư?"

"The two sisters are probably almost here. I'm sorry, there's no one here to offer you some water, Sister Sáu."

"I am no guest, Mrs. Tư? Don't worry about the water."

Mrs. Tư watched as Mrs. Sáu arranged the fruits on a plate, then asked, "Is there something you want with Thanh, Sister Sáu?"

"Well, I do have a little something to tell, Mrs. Tư."

"Let me go inside and get another chair for you. We can sit outside where it's cooler."

"Sure, let me go get it," said Mrs. Sáu as she hurriedly went inside to fetch another chair for herself. Before she could sit down, Mrs. Tư asked, "Are you looking for Thanh for something specific, Sister Sáu?"

"Well, I have a bit of news to share with you, Mrs. Tư."

Mrs. Sáu spoke in a continuous stream, leaving Mrs. Tư to suspect that Mrs. Sáu might be sizing up her daughter. Although Mrs. Tư knew that Mrs. Sáu was a professional matchmaker, she didn't expect that with only two days left before her family would leave for Saigon, she couldn't escape Mrs. Sáu. Mrs. Tư was still perplexed, unsure how to respond to Mrs. Sáu when she heard the footsteps of Thanh and Nhàn approaching the porch. Mrs. Tư called the two over to greet Mrs. Sáu:

"You two are back? Come in and greet Mrs. Sáu."

Thanh assisted Nhàn in hanging a wet cloth and two sets of clothes on the bamboo rack near some chili bushes beside the house before they stepped in front of the house to address Mrs. Sáu.

"Welcoming, Mrs. Sáu," Thanh greeted with a polite nod.

Mrs. Sáu tilted her head and laughed heartily, her mouth revealing betel nut residue at the corner. "Oh dear... very impressive indeed. City girls are truly different; even their speech is more sophisticated than others." Her eyes wandered over Thanh as she continued, "Poor Miss Thanh, being a city girl and having to endure the hardship of living in the countryside, with hands being covered in mud all day from morning till night..."

Pausing as if suddenly remembering something, Mrs. Sáu continued, "Oh, but I don't know how old you are this year."

"She's seventeen," Mrs. Tư interjected.

"Ah, so she's born in the Year of the Horse..."

Mrs. Sáu suddenly furrowed her brow, recalling Mrs. Hộ's advice to avoid the Horse year when finding a daughter-in-law because that was the year of her third daughter-in-law, who had caused so much trouble in her house. After a moment of hesitation, Mrs. Sáu reassured herself, 'Let's consider that later.' Instantly, her eyebrows relaxed, and she quickly straightened them, raising them into two arcs over her eyes like a hawk spotting a tasty prey in the night.

Smiling broadly, Mrs. Sáu inquired, "Were you born at night?"

Curious, Thanh replied, "How do you know that, Mrs. Sáu?"

Smiling knowingly, Mrs. Sáu explained, "You see, I can tell. With your fair skin, long hair, beautiful face, and elegant demeanor, you can't possibly be born at any other time. A 'Horse' person - people who are born in the year of the Horse - often has to endure hardship in their life if they were born during the day. They have to pull carriages carrying others, you know. But, a 'Horse' born before the Rooster hour, like yours, belongs to... the Celestial Horse. It's quite a different story, you know."

The two young sisters burst into laughter, prompting Mrs. Sáu to add, "Seriously, Miss Thanh, for a girl born in the Year of the Horse, she'll usually have a lot of twists and turns in her love life. At the very least, she'll have two or three husbands. For the lucky ones who can keep one husband, they would spend their whole life working tirelessly to support their husband's family. Moreover, let me tell you, for those who have unfortunately been labeled as 'Mrs. Horse' since childhood, finding a husband is nearly impossible. But for someone like you, a genuine 'Celestial Horse,' you would have it all, wealth and prosperity with servants on their hands and knees serving you, you know."

Remaining calm, Thanh responded, "Well, I find enough joy living with my parents, Mrs. Sáu."

Mrs. Tư, aware that Mrs. Sáu was leading the conversation towards matchmaking for Thanh, noticed Nhàn standing beside her young sister. While Nhàn seemed happy for her sister, there was a hint of sadness and a private sense of concern, being the older sister watching her younger sibling being approached for marriage matters first. Mrs. Tư tactfully sent the two girls to the back to prepare bundles of fabric to sell at the market tomorrow, giving her the chance to speak privately with Mrs. Sáu. "Alright, there is no place for children here. Thanh, why don't you take your sister to the back and pack the fabric into the basket, so that I can deliver it to the store at the market tomorrow."

Left alone with Mrs. Tư, Mrs. Sáu didn't waste any time. "No need for me to beat around the bush, Mrs. Tư. Mrs. Hộ in An Phú Village asked me to find a daughter-in-law for her."

Mrs. Tư interrupted, "I've also heard that Mrs. Hộ is looking for a wife for her youngest son who just finished studying in the city. The Hộ's family is wealthy, owning vast lands. There's no shortage of suitable candidates for them."

"You don't say. But until now, she hasn't found a place she's satisfied with. The reason is that since her eldest son returned from studying in France with a foreign wife, she's been fed up. That's why, for her younger son, she would like to find a local girl with French education to keep him company, avoiding the possibility of him following his older brother's footsteps by going to France and bringing back another foreign wife. But look, in these villages, the girls don't even know how to read and write our own language, let alone French. It's like destiny arranged for your daughter to come here. I believe it's predestined, not just a coincidence, Mrs. Tư."

Mrs. Tư, curious to know, "How old is Mrs. Hộ's youngest son?"

"Well, he's born in the Year of the Cat..."

Before she could finish her sentence, Mrs. Sáu suddenly realized, "Oh no, the Tiger-Monkey-Rooster-Dog clash..." At the same time, Mrs. Tư appeared to be puzzled about the same issue - the compatibility between Thanh's zodiac sign and that of Mrs. Hộ's son. Mrs. Tư quickly raised the issue, "Hmm, not quite compatible. Last year, a fortune teller in Saigon mentioned that Thanh's zodiac sign clashes with the Cat's."

"Don't worry, Mrs. Tư. It's not a big deal. I've been doing matchmaking for decades, and there is no problem here. The compatibility in this case is not perfect, but it's alright. I've arranged for many couples like this before. Don't fret; I've got it all under control. It won't be a major issue at all."

Mrs. Sáu shifted her tobacco lump from left to right and then from right to left, suddenly stopping as if she remembered something important, "Mrs. Tư, let me tell you, they may not have compatible signs, but the good thing is they do not have an 'aversion' to each other. Even when there's 'aversion,' a simple offering at the temple can turn it into 'harmony.' Actually, in reality, you don't even need to make offerings. Couples might argue in the day, but they always reconcile by nightfall. The important thing is not to keep silent and harbor grudges; that's when problems arise."

Mrs. Tư, grateful for Mrs. Sáu's generosity in bringing over four star apple fruits, had patiently listened to her stories. However, with numerous pressing household matters weighing on her mind and only two nights left before she had to return to Saigon with Thanh and Nhàn, Mrs. Tư couldn't shake a growing sense of restlessness.

Realizing the need to address the impending matchmaking discussion, Mrs. Tư spoke decisively:

"Thank you, Mrs. Sáu, for thinking of my daughter. However, my husband insists that the day after tomorrow, we must take the kids back. Perhaps we can consider your offer at another time."

Mrs. Sáu, aware of the urgency, hurriedly explained:

"Oh, Mrs. Tư, I understand you need to return to the city. That's why I rushed over to share this good news with you and Miss Thanh. The Hộ family is wealthy, with vast fields and gardens. Since they only have a younger son left to find a bride, they are very eager to welcome Miss Thanh into their family. If she marries there, I guarantee she'll be pampered without having to lift a finger. Her life will be comfortable and blissful."

As the darkness approached, Mrs. Tư interjected:

"Sister Sáu, please understand. Without my husband present, I can't make a decision about my daughter's entire life alone. Moreover, with only two days left here, it's too late to make such significant arrangements."

Mrs. Sáu reassured her:

"No worries, Mrs. Tư. I understand. Just nod your head, and tomorrow, they'll bring all the ceremonial gifts to you. Then, when you see Mr. Tư, you can discuss it with him. There's no rush."

Resigned to the situation, Mrs. Tư reluctantly nodded her head, inadvertently confirming once again that the predetermined fate of the Vietnamese woman could unfold before the matchmaker finished the lump of tobacco in her mouth. Thanh cried through the night, and, just like that, the next morning, she was declared the fiancée of the youngest son of the Hộ family in An Phú village.

2. Silent Pain

The morning light broke, and Thanh, fortified by her breakfast, reclaimed her determination. Dismissing the looming specter of an arranged marriage, she confidently strode out of her home, bidding farewell to her cloth-weaving companions. Along the narrow embankment beside a shallow ditch, she walked briskly, a purposeful gait unwarranted by any immediate urgency. Abruptly, teasing chants echoed from the rice fields being seeded:

"Ho... oh...,
Oh, the rosy-cheeked maiden,
Why won't you take a husband farmer?"

Điền, an incurable romantic, had persistently tried to propose to Thanh through his mother, yet his efforts had been in vain. Today, in this unexpected encounter, overwhelmed by his emotions, he borrowed the rhythmic chants to convey his pent-up feelings.

At the age of 15, Thanh had a family portrait taken at 'La Lumière' photo studio on Galliéni Street. After the photo's development, the shop owner sought her father's permission to enlarge Thanh's portrait for display in the shop's front window. The beauty of her youth, now enhanced by the patina of maturity acquired through months of exposure to the natural elements of the countryside, showcased the resolute features on her oval face. These were the intrinsic qualities that her friends had recognized since childhood. Though seldom seen smiling, her eyes always emitted a friendly and approachable demeanor.

Raising her bamboo leaf hat, Thanh scanned the surroundings to find Điền. Her eyes suddenly sparkled, not like the romantic moon vying for attention amidst the stars in the night sky, but akin to the morning light warming the dawn. It subtly expressed empathy for Điền, transcending the playful chants from the rice field.

Mận, a friend who was sowing seeds in the adjacent field, had harbored deep feelings for Điền for a long time, yet all she received from him was indifference. Today, she seized the opportunity to engage in playful banter with him:

"Ho... oh...,
Listen here, my dreamy brother,
Don't chase after those fancy precious flowers.
Our village is full of wild ones in the fields,
Why not pluck them and bring them home for a little... display?"

In a teasing tone, she implied that Điền's affection for his love was so intense that he might as well place her on the ancestral altar to pay respects. Điền blushed, lowering his head with a shy smile. Ngạn, a boy standing beside him, didn't let the chance for a quick retort slip away and confidently cleared his throat before chanting in response:

"Ho... oh...,
You stay right there and wait,
When we're free, we'll come over.
Clip those wildflowers down,
Bring them home... to cook with brine!"

The group of boys erupted into laughter, drowning out the feeble curses - 'Devilish creature' - from the girls. Thanh secretly rejoiced as their banter provided an escape for her. Reluctantly, she continued walking along the dyke, under the shadow of dense tamanu trees, next to the water-filled ditch. Her heart stirred with fondness for the fields, gardens, and the people closely connected to them.

At the end of the day, as the night enveloped the surroundings in darkness, Mrs. Tư and her two daughters gathered around the woven rattan trunk strategically positioned in the center of the wooden plank beside the flickering oil lamp. They were engrossed in the task of packing up the last remnants of their belongings, diligently preparing for the imminent journey to reunite with Mr. Tư.

Upon carefully placing her final possession, a pristine white 'áo dài' (traditional Vietnamese long tunic), into the trunk - a dress that had remained untouched for months - Mrs. Tư gestured for her daughters to draw closer. Lowering her voice to a hushed tone, she imparted a cautious message, "Remember, when we reunite with your father, convey to him that..."

She momentarily halted, then directed her gaze towards Nhàn, stating, "... this ordeal was brought about by the Japanese soldiers, understood?"

"Yes, Mom, I understand," Thanh responded promptly. Meanwhile, Nhàn remained huddled, her knees tightly pressed together, veiling her face in the obscurity of the night.

Mrs. Tư continued with a hint of worry in her voice. "I fear that inadvertently, you two might disclose the truth. If your father were to discover that this was done by the son of Mr. Hai, it would deeply unsettle him." Mr. Hai is one of the few remaining friends of Mr. Tư. Considering Mr. Tư's association with the French in the city, many of his village acquaintances shunned and ostracized him. Only Mr. Hai and a few steadfast friends continued to communicate with him, offering occasional visits. That's why he held them in such high regard.

Mentioning Mr. Tư, Mrs. Tư directed her gaze into the dark, contemplating her husband's current precarious situation. Thanh discreetly glanced at her sister, startled, and exclaimed, "Sister is biting her lips again!" Mrs. Tư promptly leaned forward, embracing Nhàn. Her gentle hands caressed Nhàn's cheeks, and her words of comfort didn't cease, "It's okay, my child... it's okay. Mom apologizes to you. Mom will never mention that again. It's just that mom worries about you two and fears that your father will be upset. I feel sorry for him..." Mrs. Tư choked up, hastily wiping away tears with the cloth hanging from her shoulder, then consoled her daughter, "What's done is done; try to let it go, my child."

Thanh immediately thought of Mrs. Tư's previous admonition when Nhàn bit her lip until it bled at the mention of the son of Mr. Hai. Thanh hurriedly went to prepare a glass of saltwater to help her sister rinse her mouth.

"I have to go to Uncle Hai to tell him about his son," Thanh said angrily.

Mrs. Tư gently shook her head to dissuade her, saying, "No, dear, you can't." After a thoughtful pause, she advised, "Think about it. How will Uncle Hai handle this when there's such a wicked son in the family? If this thing is exposed, he would lose face in the whole village and might have to leave his ancestral home." Mrs. Tư looked into the emptiness ahead, expressing her deep concern. "And when the news reaches your father, it will cause him immense distress."

Mrs. Tư sighed deeply, stroking Nhàn's hair for comfort, "Hold on, my child. Mom is a woman too, and Mom understands you." Hearing this, Nhàn's tears suddenly burst forth. She buried her head in her mother's shoulder, sobbing uncontrollably. Mrs. Tư held her tightly, consoling, "Hang in there, my dear... Mom knows how you feel."

At this point, Nhàn's tears flowed even more freely. She pressed her head against her mother's shoulder, crying softly. Mrs. Tư embraced her daughter, comforting, "Be strong, my child... try to endure." Her mother's arms tightened around her petite frame, conveying the sacred promise of a lifetime, "Mom will always be with you." Forever, like a quaint melody of a lullaby in the wind:

"The plank is nailed down, easy to walk on,
The bamboo bridge sways precariously, difficult to cross
Difficult to cross, but mom guides the way
... As you go to school, mom enters the school of life."

If school teaches the daughter the three obediences and four virtues, then life teaches the mother cultivated with patience and endurance. Mrs. Tư gazed into the undefined space and murmured softly, "Endure, my child." The advice to her daughter seemed like a reminder to herself, to be strong and resilient in the face of the unpredictable storm always waiting somewhere for a woman.

In the darkness, Thanh, her sister, and mother struggled to find sleep. Thanh felt her sister's worries, becoming restless with anxiety. She kept tossing and turning under the invisible pressures closing in on her. Silently, she prayed that all the storms in life would soon pass. Next to her, Mrs. Tư didn't cease to blame herself for not fulfilling her duty as a mother. She ran her fingers through Nhàn's hair, tenderly resolving the tangles as she had done countless times before since misfortune befell Nhàn: "It's Mom's fault. Seeing you two with pimples, Mom went to Aunt Tám's garden in the neighboring hamlet to pick some remedial herbs, leaving you alone at home that noon."

Mrs. Tư couldn't bring herself to close her eyes, absentmindedly staring into the silent space within their home, anxious about the fate of her children in the impending journey ahead.

3. The Quartet of Colette

Mr. Tư was relocated to a position in the Bãi Sậy region, situated on the outskirts of Saigon city. Despite its remote and desolate nature, this location held significant strategic importance for the French authorities. The Bãi Sậy police station was established outside Cây Lý hamlet, more than 10 kilometers southwest of the city center, with the primary objective of preventing anti-French resistance forces from the Western provinces from infiltrating Saigon. Once Mr. Tư became acquainted with the new area and settled into a routine with his police work, he sent word for his wife and their two daughters to join him for a long-awaited family reunion.

Mr. Tư warmly welcomed his family to a police officer compound in Bãi Sậy. The compound comprised a series of single-story houses tailored for Vietnamese employees and their families, discreetly nestled behind a row of multi-story residences facing the river. These taller buildings served as the residence for French personnel and other Vietnamese officials with French nationality.

On the day of their long-awaited reunion, amid a heavy downpour, the police compound witnessed a sudden break in the clouds. Sunlight streamed through, casting a shimmering welcome to Thanh and her family.

Thanh barely returned to Saigon, and the next day, her three closest friends came to visit. Mỹ Lệ, Dung, and Loan (You can call them Mee Lei, Yung, and Loanne respectively), together with Thanh, used to be known as the quartet from Colette Primary School in the past. They gathered around the dining table in Thanh's kitchen, chatting and laughing joyfully to compensate for the days of separation. After four years of schooling at Colette and experiencing the sweet and bitter moments of youth, they became inseparable friends, bonded like family despite their different circumstances and backgrounds.

The story among the four sisters quickly shifted to an inevitable topic during every reunion: Love. The first 'victim' of every teasing and inquisitive gaze this time was Dung. With her round face, honey-like skin, sweet as the fruits of the Mekong Delta, and without any makeup except for her sparkling almond-shaped eyes, Dung carried a lingering melancholy from her past in the vast distant horizon. Thanh glanced in Dung's direction, seated next to her, and asked curiously,

"What about you and 'brother' Án?"

"Well, you know, parents decide where their children should sit."

Mỹ Lệ, the eldest among the four sisters, teased her younger 'sister':

"Come on, if parents decide to place you somewhere else, would you agree?"

Turning to Thanh, Mỹ Lệ squinted one eye, "She loves him to death. Just pretending to be cool."

Loan jumped in to defend Dung. She asked Mỹ Lệ:

"Stop poking at Dung. What about you and Sứ?"

With her hair elevated like two waves caressing a boat, Mỹ Lệ responded with a dismissive smirk, a habitual expression borrowed from the colonial French, suggesting '*On s'en fout*' (We don't care). Despite her seemingly indifferent attitude towards life, it's her clear and bright eyes, often widening to reveal genuine interest in friends, that betray her disguise. In reality, those eyes reflect an underlying resilience ready to cast aside any lingering concerns about matters she deems as trivial, such as romantic affairs.

As if remembering something, Thanh curiously asked Mỹ Lệ:

"Oh right, before I left the city, I had heard you two wanted to get married. What happened to that?"

Loan jumped in to reproach,

"Not just for you Thanh, even for us. We were here with her, but she still keeps us in the dark."

Mỹ Lệ hesitated before whispering that her boyfriend Sứ had joined the Việt Minh, an organization that led a struggle against French rule. While Sứ's friends joined the resistance groups in the countryside, Sứ was ordered to set up a stall selling sunglasses near Saigon Market as a '*sleeping cell*,' serving as a messaging center for the organization.

Pondering for a moment, Mỹ Lệ recounted for the first time to her friends:

"My father found out, and he almost died worrying... The marriage plans are as good as impossible."

The group sympathized with Mỹ Lệ's dilemma, gathered to console her, but again she brushed it off with a French shrug - *C'est la vie* (That's life). Suddenly, she smirked mysteriously:

"Who says you can't be married without a wedding ceremony."

The three sisters were stunned by Mỹ Lệ's bold suggestion, even though she may be half-joking. With Mỹ Lệ's determination, known to all, nothing seemed impossible once she set her mind to it. Loan expressed her admiration and sympathy to Mỹ Lệ, rather than giving advice or trying to stop her, although in Loan's mind, it was an unimaginable thing for her to contemplate. Thanh felt the need to steer the conversation away to avoid putting Mỹ Lệ in an awkward situation and turned to tease Loan:

"You are good at talking about others, but what about your relationship with Hùng?"

Hùng, Mỹ Lệ's brother, was once Loan's *hero* until a day when her parents forbade her from meeting him, deeming him unworthy of their daughter. Loan, the daughter of a Provincial Chief - an esteemed government position reserved by the French authorities for a Vietnamese - exuded an air of aristocracy despite her youth. Though her friends dubbed her a *princess,* her straightforward nature drew criticism for not aligning with traditional notions of nobility.

The wound in Loan's heart from her first love lingered, a fact known well to Mỹ Lệ, who maintained her friendship with Loan. To prevent any unintentional remarks that might make Loan uncomfortable, Mỹ Lệ turned to Thanh jokingly and asked,

"And what about you? Have you encountered any White Princes or Black Princes (referring to the two legendary wealthy landowner sons of the time) during your months in the countryside?"

Thanh sealed her lips, pretending to harbor a secret that couldn't be revealed, but eventually, she couldn't keep it to herself any longer:

"I have been committed."

Everyone rushed to express their thoughts; some blamed Thanh, while others threatened to 'break up' with her for breaking their oath of not keeping secrets from each other. Thanh calmly responded,

"Relax, relax. That was just a thing of the past. There was a 'beau prince' who proposed through a matchmaker, and my mom was forced by circumstances, so... yeah. But as soon as I got back here, I settled things with my dad. He's having someone return all the gifts to them."

The whole group breathed a sigh of relief, but Mỹ Lệ pressed on to make sure:

"So, you're still '*célibataire*' (single)?"

"*Oui, madame*... Yes, ma'am. Are you satisfied?"

Time passed quickly when people have fun. Before parting ways, Thanh asked, 'Who wants to visit my mom's tomb with me tomorrow?'

"What month is it now? I thought the Tomb-Sweeping Day passed a while ago," Dung asked.

"Yeah, but I missed visiting my mom's grave last year..."

Thanh trailed off, expressing her longing for her late mother.

4. Tomb-Sweeping Day

Thanh woke up long before dawn to prepare the offering for her mother's memorial. She meticulously filled each compartment of the '*gamelle*,' a lunch box consisting of four stacking pails, to carry it to the cemetery. In the bottom pail, she placed rice and spread a layer of shredded fish floss on top, prepared from a snakehead fish by her own hands since yesterday. This dish was her mother's favorite during her lifetime, and since Thanh knew how to cook, she never forgot to make it as an offering on Tomb-Sweeping Days.

The third compartment held four plums and a cluster of chili salt for dipping. In front of Thanh's old house, there was a Vietnamese plum tree with bell-shaped fruits that, during rare leisure times, her mother would pick to share with her. Thanh fondly remembered how her mother would cut each plum in half before giving it to her, ensuring she wouldn't inadvertently eat any with worms inside. As for her mother, she would simply bite into the fruit after dipping it in chili salt. These were rare moments that made Thanh feel truly happy being with her mother.

The two top compartments of the '*gamelle*' were temporarily left empty, reserved for slices of roasted pork and sauces that Thanh planned to buy on her way at the market near her friend's home. Thanh carefully placed the '*gamelle*' in her handbag along with a bundle of incense sticks, two candles, and a box of matches.

Thanh walked from her house to the bridge at the end of the street to catch a ride to the Xóm Củi market. From there, she walked for another 15 minutes across the Chà Và bridge to the front of the Chợ Lớn Post Office, where she caught a bus to meet Dung and Mỹ Lệ, who were waiting for her at Mỹ Lệ's house. The three 'sisters' then set off together.

Earlier, Thanh had also stopped by the Ông Lãnh's Bridge market to buy 500 grams of roast pork and two loaves of bread, which were part of the offering for her mother but also served as lunch for them afterward. Thanh intentionally brought an ample supply of 'provisions' because she also intended to share the food with Uncle Năm, a cemetery caretaker, in appreciation for his and his family's care of the tomb of her mother.

Outside the gate of the cemetery, Uncle Năm was sitting on a plank in front of his house, whittling a new fishing rod. Upon hearing footsteps outside, he looked up and instantly recognized Thanh. He quickly set aside his tools, ran to the gate, and greeted her:

"Is this Miss Thanh? Long time no see. How have you been, Miss Thanh?"

Since Thanh had been accompanying her father to attend her mother's memorial every year, she had become a familiar face to Uncle Năm. Thanh was also happy to meet him. She replied:

"I'm well, thank you, Uncle Năm. You, Aunty Năm, and Brother Rê are also well?"

"Thanks to heaven, our family is fine. The only thing is... in this wartime, not many people come here for ceremonial things. Except when they have to come here to bury their deceased relatives, you hardly see anyone around here. It's usually deserted."

"Last year I was evacuated to my father's hometown, so I couldn't come," Thanh explained.

"Oh, Miss Thanh, don't worry. Every year, my son and I take care of cleaning Mrs. Tư's grave, whether you and Mr. Tư come or not."

Thanh expressed her gratitude to Uncle Năm and followed him to pay a visit to her mother's resting place. The cemetery was dotted with dirt mounds, both large and small, each representing the final resting place of ordinary people in this part of the city. Few ventured here regularly to tend to the graves of their departed loved ones, especially during challenging times.

Uncle Năm took the lead, skillfully wielding his machete to clear a path through the overgrown grass. As they approached, the evidence of recent care for Thanh's mother's grave became apparent. The surrounding areas were dominated by tall weeds, but her mother's tomb stood out with fewer obtrusive plants, and the inscription on the tombstone retained its vibrant red hue, evidence of a recent coat of paint.

Driven by a sense of routine, Uncle Năm reached over the tomb to remove a few lingering vines, then stooped down to meticulously clear every tuft of grass beneath his feet. Thanh surveyed the well-tended grave of her mother, a sense of satisfaction settling within her. She expressed her gratitude once again to Uncle Năm for his thoughtful care.

As Dung and Mỹ Lệ arranged the offerings on the stone tablet at the base of the tombstone, Thanh stood beside them, her gaze fixed on her mother's name engraved on the tombstone. After a brief moment of reflection, she turned to Uncle Năm and spoke,

"Uncle Năm, may I borrow the can of red paint and a brush to apply another coat on the letters on the tombstone? I know you've already taken care of it, but since it might be a few more months before I return, I want to refresh the paint for my mother while I'm here."

"Of course, Miss Thanh," replied Uncle Năm as he left to retrieve the paint supplies.

Meanwhile, the group was disturbed by teasing shouts emanating from a nearby French outpost. Two Senegalese soldiers, African mercenaries hired by the French, were watering a vegetable garden behind a barbed wire fence. They pointed fingers, laughed, and shouted in the direction of Thanh and her companions. Unsettled by the situation, Thanh urged her friends,

"Let's light the incense and candles and then leave, guys."

Dung, clutching a bundle of incense sticks, swiftly planted them into the sand-filled can positioned in front of the grave. Mỹ Lệ couldn't help but mockingly chuckle,

"Look at her. The incense isn't even lit, and no one has prayed yet, but she's already stuck them in."

Remaining composed, Mỹ Lệ struck a match, igniting two candles. She carefully dripped wax onto the stone tablet, securing the candles in place. In a calm but authoritative tone, she issued the order,

"Let's expedite the ceremony and leave. It's not safe to linger here."

Keeping a watchful eye on the reactions of the two African soldiers, Dung suddenly whispered,

"They're coming this way."

Fortuitously, as Uncle Năm approached his house, he caught wind of the commotion from the French outpost. Exercising caution, he summoned his son to accompany him, and they hastened towards Thanh and her friends for protection.

Uncle Năm was merely taking precautions, having developed an acquaintance with the soldiers at the outpost over the past few months. Since the Japanese army overthrew the French authorities and assumed control of Vietnam, the French soldiers had been disarmed. While some French soldiers in the South fled into the jungle in search of a route to neighboring Cambodia, most remained in place - either guiding the Japanese forces around unfamiliar territories or identifying resistance elements to them.

The outpost, once manned by nearly 20 personnel, mostly Vietnamese soldiers, had seen a significant departure. Only a handful of scar-faced African soldiers and a French lieutenant named Paul, who had joined them from an undisclosed location, remained. They sporadically visited the village, ostensibly requesting fruits but, in reality, probing for information about the activities of the Vietnamese resistance to relay to the Japanese army.

As the three sisters raced halfway to Uncle Năm's house, a scar-faced soldier managed to catch up, just as Uncle Năm and his son arrived. Swiftly, they blocked the soldier's path with their machetes. Given the frequent coconut-sharing history between the soldier and Uncle Năm's family, they engaged in casual conversation with the sisters. The soldier, expressing a desire for a friendly chat, remarked that it had been a while since he last encountered a beautiful city girl. Sensing the tension, Mỹ Lệ, quick-witted, exchanged pleasantries with him in French.

Amidst their conversation, Paul arrived. He had been bathing when he heard a soldier's report and hurried to prevent his men from disturbing the villagers. Apologizing for his lack of time to don a shirt, he stood before them in khaki shorts, revealing a chest covered in hair. His face, concealed by a bushy red beard, left only two sparkling blue eyes filled with curiosity visible.

After Paul signaled for the scar-faced soldiers to return to the outpost, he apologized, saying, "I'm sorry that they have disturbed you all." Thanh reassured him, "It's okay. Maybe they just wanted to make friends when they saw strangers."

Paul inquired further, "Is today a special day? Are you here to visit your loved one's grave?"

"Yes, I'm visiting my mother's grave with my two friends here," Thanh responded. Paul extended his hand to shake Thanh's and introduced himself, "I'm Paul. And you?"

After the three sisters introduced themselves, Paul continued, "Where are you all from?" Quick-witted as always, Mỹ Lệ replied, "We live in the Xây-nho police housing area, and Thanh lives in the Bãi Sậy police quarter." Mỹ Lệ's intention was to subtly convey that their families worked for the French government, in case Paul had any ulterior motives. However, he raised an eyebrow while looking at Mỹ Lệ.

Following a brief silence, Paul suggested talking privately with Mỹ Lệ and asked everyone else to proceed to Uncle Năm's house first. Thanh hesitated, reluctant to leave her friend alone, but then heard Paul ask Mỹ Lệ, "Are you Mr. Sáu's daughter?" Surprised, Thanh assumed they already knew each other, prompting her to pull Dung with her.

Mỹ Lệ asked,

"Yes, how do you know?"

"I used to work at the Xây-nho police station for a short time. Do you remember me?"

Mỹ Lệ suspected she had encountered Paul before but thought it might be because he resembled Jacques, the Chief Police's son, who had been pursuing her for a while.

"I'm sorry, I don't remember meeting you anywhere."

"Try to recall, on the night the Japanese military took power, was there a stranger hiding in your house?"

Mỹ Lệ finally remembered:

"Ah, you drank with my father that evening and stayed overnight at my house. You slept on the plank behind the kitchen."

"Yes, thanks to your father for hiding me for one night."

Paul spoke with a sly tone before continuing:

"And only until noon the next day, the Japanese soldiers came and arrested me. Do you know how they found out my whereabouts so quickly?"

"Sorry, it was unfortunate for you, but I don't know how they knew."

"It was your father who informed the Japanese authority that morning."

"I really didn't know about that. In the afternoon, my father was also detained by the Japanese. If he did that, it was only to protect the family, and I'm sure you understand the suffering of my family. We are all victims of the circumstances."

Paul raised his voice:

"I can understand that, but I just asked him to let me stay for two days so I could contact a friend to find my way to Cambodia."

"I sincerely apologize."

"What's the point of apologizing now? I was arrested and tortured for two days, and locked up in solitary confinement for a month. I should have known not to trust the deceitful Annamites."

Upon hearing Paul use such a derogatory term for the Vietnamese, Mỹ Lệ slapped him hard across the face and shouted loudly,

"You cannot insult my people. Whatever happened, it's only between you and my family."

Enraged and with a red face, he glared at Mỹ Lệ and yelled,

"Fine. I know you Annamites are very proud. Let me teach you a lesson, show you who's in charge in this wretched land."

He grabbed Mỹ Lệ by the throat until she almost passed out and proceeded to assault her.

5. The Surrogate Mother

Despite the Japanese Emperor's declaration of unconditional surrender following the U.S. dropping two atomic bombs that devastated the major cities of Hiroshima and Nagasaki, not all Japanese forces withdrew from Vietnam. Some resorted to harakiri, a traditional act of self-disembowelment, driven by the samurai spirit. Others, fueled by intense nationalism and skepticism towards news of Japan's defeat, chose to stay in Vietnam. Furthermore, they adopted the Greater East Asia Co-Prosperity Sphere ideology, advocating 'Asia for Asians,' and retreated into the mountainous regions of Vietnam to support the Vietnamese resistance against the French.

These scattered forces, while not numerous, emerged concurrently with various armed factions, competing for influence to fill the power vacuum left by the French and Japanese military. Disorder permeated the region, stemming not only from conflicts between opposing forces but also from lethal internal disputes within certain martial factions. The situation grew increasingly complex, and the future direction of the country remained uncertain.

The "*Motherland*" of France found itself depleted due to the aftermath of World War II. The French colonial apparatus in Indochina virtually collapsed after being under Japanese control. Consequently, the Allies tasked England with the responsibility of stabilizing the situation in Indochina, given the British military's extensive experience in colonial governance across Asia, from India to Malaya, and from Singapore to Indochina. As a result, another piece on the geopolitical chessboard in Vietnam was introduced: England.

At the local coffee shop, Mr. Tư sat at a table with his friends and colleagues, appearing quieter than usual. He voiced his concerns, saying, "I wonder if the English plan to replace the French permanently and what their intentions are here."

Sergeant Cừ, a feared figure in Cây Lý's hamlet, sighed reluctantly and added, "I haven't finished learning French yet. Where can I find my English to work for those English bosses? Or, worst of all, what if they bring in their own people to replace us?"

Teacher Hai, a respected figure known for his broad knowledge, attempted to console the two French workers with a half-joking tone, saying, "Relax, gentlemen. There's nothing to worry about. In this urgent situation, they won't replace you. Where would they find people to help them suppress these 'rebel forces' during the crisis?"

However, Sergeant Cừ remained uneasy and asked Teacher Hai, "I heard that General Soái in the army of the Hòa Hảo's Buddhist sect is siding with the French. Is that true, Teacher?"

"Well, it's said that he has a joint agreement with Colonel Cluzet," replied Teacher Hai.

Curious, Cừ inquired about the plans of the army from the Cao Đài Buddhist sect. Teacher Hai admitted, "I can only guess. I don't know the details of their affairs."

Teacher Hai shook his head in frustration, reflecting on how the political maneuvers of the "rebel forces" had brought discord to the religious sects, tarnishing the reputation of the two major religions born in the South. These venerable homegrown religions, deeply rooted in local culture, should be cherished, if not embraced.

Mr. Tư grumbled as he rode his bike home, burdened by personal worries. His eldest daughter, Nhàn, was about to give birth. Since last night, his wife had reminded him to be prepared to go to the neighborhood and bring the midwife, Mrs. Mười, to assist with the delivery.

Seven months after returning to the city with her mother and disabled sister, Thanh had to face yet another tragedy that marked a fateful turn in her life.

It was pouring rain, and from afternoon to dusk, there was no sign of it letting up. Inside Mr. Tư's house, nestled within the police compound, Mrs. Mười, a midwife, anxiously awaited signs of labor. Despite her vigilance, there were no indications yet. Mrs. Tư, gauging Nhàn's expressions, occasionally raised her voice in alarm, "It must be coming, Mrs. Mười." Drawing on her experience, Mrs. Mười knew it was still early, and a few more hours of waiting were inevitable. Seeking permission, she excused herself to attend to personal matters.

Before departing, Mrs. Mười reassured everyone that Nhàn's childbirth was in its early stages and posed a challenge due to being her first delivery - her body not accustomed to the process. "By next time," Mrs. Mười added optimistically, "she would push it out in no time."

Shortly after the midwife left, Mrs. Tư panicked, exclaiming, "Her water has broken, my goodness!" Mr. Tư, glancing at the swinging clock, showed a concerned expression, realizing it was already deep into the night. Despite the rain having ceased, going out at this hour was perilous, especially into the neighborhood outside the walls of the police compound during this chaotic period. Nevertheless, with his daughter's life at stake, Mr. Tư hesitated not. Grabbing the prepared flashlight from the bedside table and, out of habit, securing the revolver in his belt, he hastily stepped out the door to fetch the midwife.

Unfortunately, upon his return, it was too late. The midwife could only save one of the two lives. Nhàn's life could not be preserved, and she departed permanently as the unfortunate daughter of Mr. and Mrs. Tư.

In memory of Nhàn's filial piety towards her parents, despite living most of her life with an illness, Mr. Tư chose the name Thảo for his orphaned granddaughter from the moment she entered the world. Thanh, a young girl at the age of dreams, overwhelmed by a sense of duty, took on the responsibility of raising her niece in place of her late sister.

6. Facing the Devil

The United Kingdom and France, despite being allies and neighbors separated only by a narrow sea channel, carried a long and complex history of conflict and rivalry. Consequently, the British government did not wholeheartedly support France in consolidating its colonial rule in Vietnam, as had been entrusted to them by the Allies of World War Two. After reluctantly undertaking the task of stabilizing Indochina for six months, the British army silently withdrew from Vietnam.

The colonial French authorities hastily reestablished themselves, resembling 'a child abandoned at the market forced to find its own way to survive.' French officials employed all the cunning tactics they had previously used, creating divisions between different factions of armed forces opposing the French. The French authorities manipulated these groups to eliminate one another through various deceitful alliances. Additionally, they provided backing to criminal gangs operating casinos, opium dens, and other notorious entertainment venues as a form of economic support for their military.

Among the infamous gang leaders was Năm Chảng, a 'Big Brother' who led a group of gangsters in his territory around Saigon Market. Năm Chảng's towering figure, measuring more than seven feet in height, was sufficient to inspire awe among his underlings. With a neck as massive as a bull's neck, carrying above a pair of stern, glaring eyes that could easily intimidate an unfortunate opponent. However, this did not mean he lacked intelligence; he was a cunning and resourceful individual.

The origin of his formidable nickname, "Năm Chảng," served as evidence. Originally named Hổ (Tiger) because he was born in the Year of the Tiger, the fifth child in a poor peasant family, Năm Chảng found his claim to fame at the age of seventeen. A large wild buffalo frequently invaded the village, causing havoc during the harvest season. Despite villagers' desperate prayers to the hidden spirits and Buddhas for the buffalo to leave, it persisted. In order to show gratitude and avoid offending the buffalo's spirit, the villagers respectfully referred to it as "Ông Chảng," or "Mr. Huge." Despite the reverence, "Ông Chảng" continued to return to the village to forage.

In the midst of villagers' helplessness, not knowing what to do, young Hổ secretly devised a plan to kill "Ông Chảng." He ventured into the forest, chopped off a ton of rattan sticks, and brought them back to the village, rolling them into bundles the size of a basket. When "Ông Chảng" returned to the village, Hổ confronted it with four bundles of rattan. Each time "Ông Chảng" lunged forward, Hổ threw a bundle of rattan at it. The buffalo jabbed its horns at the bundle of rattan each time in response. Eventually, the bundles of rattan got entangled around both of the buffalo's horns, rendering its most dangerous weapon ineffective. Hổ cautiously approached and struck its neck with a machete until the buffalo collapsed. This miraculous feat later earned him the nickname "Năm Chảng" in the underworld, and the tale followed him into the realm of gangsters, garnering respect from his followers.

In Saigon, despite the scorching sun of summer, it was also the season of the Royal Poinciana, aptly named the 'student' flowers, vying for attention in the schoolyard and along the bustling streets. The vibrant red flamboyant blooms in front of Saigon

Market infused life into the already lively gathering place, while passersby entering and exiting the Saigon-Mỹ Tho train station couldn't help but be uplifted by the scene.

Over three years after the tragic events unfolded in Mỹ Lệ, her father succumbed to a severe illness. With the assistance of a relative, she secured a position as a *'planton,'* an office courier, at the Indochina Locomotive Company. Six months of dedicated work, coupled with her cheerful demeanor and resourcefulness, led to Mỹ Lệ's promotion to a clerk selling train tickets at the bustling Saigon station.

Amidst the constant flow of people, Năm Chảng noticed Mỹ Lệ. He was sitting enjoying beer in front of the Kim Điệp ice cream shop across from the train station on Lê Lai Street. Struck by love at first sight when he saw Mỹ Lệ in a pink dress, revealing her slender white thighs as she hurriedly rode her bicycle to work, he immediately instructed his two subordinates to investigate her background.

Five minutes later, after one of his henchmen returned to report on Mỹ Lệ's workplace, Năm Chảng confronted her in front of the train ticket counter. Her long, well-proportioned face, with a complexion as fair as that of a pomelo flower, left him astonished. He asked to buy a ticket to Mỹ Tho. She calmly looked at him and continued her duties as a ticket seller. He felt a bit disappointed for not eliciting the timid and fearful reaction he was used to seeing from anyone he encountered, especially from women.

Mỹ Lệ asked for the fare, and Năm Chảng's subordinate standing behind him reached the counter to pay. She accepted the money, took a ticket, punched it, and handed it to Năm Chảng. He looked at her, and as Mỹ Lệ raised an eyebrow, she asked "Do you need anything else, sir?"

My Lệ's calm and almost indifferent demeanor intrigued Năm Chảng, and he smirked, changing his tactics.

"I'm here to buy a ticket, of course, not to flirt with you, right?" he retorted.

She burst into laughter. Her innocent face exuded friendliness. She seemed approachable. Feeling a sudden interest, Năm Chảng grinned smugly and decided to alter his strategy.

"I want to buy a ticket to Mỹ Tho," he declared.

"I just sold you one," she replied.

"Now I want to buy another one. Can I?"

Looking down at the counter, Mỹ Lệ repeated the ticket-selling routine. Năm Chảng observed each of her movements, nodding in approval at the 'trophy' he was determined to have.

Holding two train tickets in his hand, he waved at Mỹ Lệ from a distance. "See you in a few days." He took a few steps and handed the two tickets to his henchman, to resell and make some coffee money.

The following day, he discovered that Mỹ Lệ resided with her elderly mother and a three-year-old Eurasian son. Năm Chảng opted to employ a familiar strategy, one he had successfully used on at least two prior occasions. He directed his subordinates to present daily gifts to Mỹ Lệ's mother, ranging from two kilograms of pork ribs to a snakehead fish or a chicken - enough to ensure indulgent meals for the family. After a week of such gestures, he approached, bearing a ceremonial tray adorned with betel-nut and three jewelry boxes. These boxes held a jade bracelet, a gold necklace, and a three-carat diamond ring - a grand proposal for marriage.

While Năm Chảng's previous overwhelming proposal tactics had never failed, this time Mỹ Lệ imposed a condition. She insisted that Năm Chảng personally assist her in seeking retribution against the French lieutenant who had assaulted her. Having tracked his movements, she knew Paul had been discharged and was now representing the Peugeot car company located on Norodom Boulevard in front of Saigon Zoo. Though typically averse to others dictating terms to him, the compelling force of love drove Năm Chảng to defy his own principles.

Less than a week later, as the driver crossed the Y-shaped bridge, Đực, Năm Chảng's loyal henchman, occupied the front seat. He pulled a revolver from his hip holster and handed it to Mỹ Lệ. "Sister Năm, this is from Brother Năm," he said, using the familial term even though Mỹ Lệ was not yet the wife of the gang leader. Mỹ Lệ gazed at the revolver in Đực's hand, raising her eyebrows in surprise. Although she had instructed Năm Chảng to allow her to personally deal with the "wicked Frenchman," facing a lethal weapon for the first time, she couldn't help but recoil in shock. Đực quickly reassured her, "It's easy, sister. When you meet him, I'll load the bullets for you. Just aim at his head, squeeze the trigger once, and he'll be dead before he can gasp. Try holding it now to get used to it."

Mỹ Lệ hesitated, but she took the revolver; unexpectedly, it was much heavier than she had anticipated. Instinctively, she clung tightly to the gun. A chill ran through her body, and her hands became sweaty. The fears that had haunted Mỹ Lệ since childhood, believed to be buried and forgotten, suddenly surged back like a nightmare in broad daylight. In Mỹ Lệ's ears, she heard the horrifying screams of tortured prisoners emanating from the second-floor windows of the Xây-nho's police headquarter. These sounds had crossed the barrier wall more than once, reaching the ears of six-year-old Mỹ Lệ as she played in the garden below.

The last time her babysitter took Mỹ Lệ to the playground was when the woman had to rush to cover Mỹ Lệ's ears after a deafening explosion on the other side of the unfeeling wall. However, in vain, the small hands of the babysitter couldn't conceal all the cruel evidence of the world's brutality. It was accumulating in Mỹ Lệ's subconscious, gnawing at her childhood.

Mỹ Lệ stared out of the car window, delving into her own forbidden memories. The furrowed brow on her father's face, the apprehensive gaze of her mother, the hushed conversations, and the masked anxiety or pretended normalcy during meals following news of someone's demise - whether a close acquaintance or a distant figure. The question of 'who killed and why' was never openly addressed; instead, it lingered as unspoken inquiries in the minds of children. Each passing day, adults silently comprehended, while children persisted in their contemplations.

The image of a battered figure suddenly rushed into Mỹ Lệ's sight. It was pulled up, lying supine on the grass, its swollen body beneath the black fabric, a purplish face, two swollen eyes shut, providing a feast for the flies buzzing around. In the innocent mind of the child, all those horrifying things originated from the object she held in her hand. It was the perpetrator of torture, murder, live burials, and throwing people into the river to drown. She detested it and wanted to throw it away.

"He's here, sister," Đực's voice snapped her back to reality. The car came to a halt outside the perimeter walls of the Ba Son shipyard, a French shipbuilding and repair facility nestled near the Saigon commercial port at Bạch Đằng Wharf - a historic cradle of the anti-French revolution for the Vietnamese workforce. Guiding Mỹ Lệ through the rows of stilt houses where the workers resided, Đực led her to the desolate warehouse at the rear. Once inside, a barren space unfolded, marked only by a handful of concrete columns supporting the roof. At the farthest column, deep within, Paul was bound, his head hanging limp against his chest, eyes shut; his whole body seemed devoid of life.

His once tall and imposing figure now resembled a stretched piece of animal hide, adorned with numerous purplish bruises and bloody whip marks across his bare chest. It was precisely as Năm Chảng had desired. On the day they apprehended Paul, Năm Chảng, eager to appease 'his lady,' had instructed his henchmen: 'Inflict a brutal beating upon him, but ensure he clings to life.' Now, it seems that the consequences have had a reverse effect; by the instinct of a compassionate person, Mỹ Lệ suddenly felt a pang of pity. However, recalling the humiliation she had endured at his hands, Mỹ Lệ angrily pointed the gun at Paul, shouting (in French): 'Why? Why?'

Paul slowly raised his head. As he lifted his eyelids, he was surprised to recognize Mỹ Lệ and hastily stammered:

"I deeply regret it, I sincerely apologize."

As Mỹ Lệ looked at him, she was stunned to see a face that was too familiar. The high, slender nose and the long, curving eyelashes always seemed to bring a smile to the sparkling eyes behind them. She could not have been mistaken. It was the face she had cherished, loved, and pampered for the past three years. It was her son, Sáng. "Father and son look so alike," she whispered to herself, even though Paul's eyes now looked tired and despondent after a day of torture. The fiery hatred in Mỹ Lệ's heart was suddenly extinguished without reason. How could she bring herself to kill a face that had been the meaning of her life for the past few years... until today, and would be forever in the remaining days.

Mỹ Lệ gazed at the gun in her hand, a sense of confusion washing over her. Hesitatingly, she spoke:

"You've ruined my life, do you realize that?"

"I know, I know. I've wronged you so much. Whatever you choose to do, I just hope you can eventually find it in your heart to forgive me."

"It's too late. My father died because of you!" Mỹ Lệ shouted vehemently.

Her father felt profound sadness upon discovering that Paul, laying blame on him, had directed all his anger towards his only daughter. Faced with unrelenting upheavals in the country and his personal life, he found himself powerless. To escape his sorrows, he turned to alcohol, and eventually, succumbed to an illness that claimed his life.

Paul whispered:

"I truly regret hearing the sad news about your father and the great loss to your family. I wish I could do something to alleviate your pain and your family's."

"We don't need anything from you..."

Before finishing her sentence, Mỹ Lệ burst into tears, dropping the gun, turning her head away from Paul's gaze, and covering her face as she sobbed. Paul mumbled, his words stumbling:

"I'm sorry... I'm so sorry. If anything I said has hurt you, please forgive me."

Mỹ Lệ's heart cried out, 'Do you know we had a child together?' but the words didn't come out; they choked in Mỹ Lệ's throat. She quickly turned away, heading toward the rays of sunlight streaming through the rusted iron door.

Đực stood outside, smoking and waiting. Surprised by the absence of gunshots, Đực asked, "Hey, why haven't I heard anything, sis?" Mỹ Lệ didn't respond; her gaze fixed beyond the shade of the old jackfruit tree canopy in front of the warehouse door. Her face was uplifted, bathing in the vast, vibrant blue sky and the radiant pink sunlight above. Đực hastily ran inside to observe, and disappointment marked his return with a gun in hand: "Sis, shall I finish it off for you?"

"No," Mỹ Lệ suddenly shouted. Đực, startled, "Why, sis? If I release him, maybe Brother Năm will kill me. He spent a lot to catch him." The more Đực spoke, the more he felt anxious about being held accountable by his boss for messing up the assignment. Without saying a word, he rushed back into the warehouse to complete the job on Paul. Mỹ Lệ panicked and ran after him, shouting, "Don't... don't... don't do that."

A black Traction, a vehicle often associated with the French secret police, sped into the Ba Son shipyard, screeching to a stop on the asphalt. It swirled onto the shoulder of the road, kicking up a cloud of dust, and finally came to a halt next to Đực's vehicle, startling the drowsy driver inside. Sensing danger, Đực quickly pulled Mỹ Lệ into the warehouse, closed the door, and stood ready with a gun in hand. It wasn't until he heard Năm Chảng's voice outside that Đực let out a sigh of relief, anxiously unlocking and swinging open the door.

Following Năm Chảng, a Frenchman in a faded white suit hurriedly entered with an anxious look. In broken Vietnamese, he asked, 'Where's Paul... Where's Paul?' Đực ushered them deeper inside, and as soon as the man saw Paul, he rushed to embrace him, murmuring into his ear, "Thank God, you're still alive." This man was none other than Captain Gauthier, the head of the Intelligence Services, operating under the alias 'Deuxième Bureau.' His name instilled fear among the public and resentment among those resisting French rule. After being discharged from the military, Paul had secretly worked for the bureau, concealing his identity behind a Peugeot car dealership.

Năm Chảng signaled to his men to untie Paul. Captain Gauthier led Paul out to the car. Mỹ Lệ watched as if she had just finished watching a movie on a screen. No resentment, no sorrow, only a sense of being free at last. Everything had come and gone. Following Năm Chảng, she stepped into the car. On the way home, Mỹ Lệ thought of her son, longing to hold him in her arms and say, 'Mom just met your father.' She suddenly bit her lip, trying to hold back the tears welling up, silently whispering, 'He's still too young to know what he needs to know.'

7. The Awaited Dawn

On a serene Sunday morning, Mỹ Lệ felt a sudden urge to bring her child to visit Thanh. Thanh was engrossed in reviewing the payroll ledger of workers at the bureau when Lý, the maid, hurriedly entered the room to announce, "Miss, Aunt Mỹ Lệ has come to visit."

Recently, a wealthy friend of Thanh's father had persuaded him to invest in a business venture. They embarked on the project of demolishing the walls of an abandoned rice warehouse to sell the debris to construction companies. The 'two old men,' as they humorously referred to themselves, had entrusted the entire management of labor to Thanh, making her quite occupied in recent times.

Despite her hectic schedule, Thanh always found joy in meeting Mỹ Lệ. Among their close circle of friends, Mỹ Lệ was perhaps the closest. This connection wasn't only because of the incident during the funeral trip that left Thanh feeling guilty, but also because Mỹ Lệ, with her elder sister personality, consistently stood ready to protect her friends as if they were her own siblings. This admirable quality both impressed and endeared Mỹ Lệ to Thanh.

Mỹ Lệ and Thanh enjoyed playing with each other's children for a while before Thanh asked Lý to take Sáng and Thảo outside to play in the garden. This allowed the two sisters to spend some quality time together. Today, Mỹ Lệ intended to confide in Thanh about the tumultuous meeting with Paul. Initially, she felt that the encounter had freed her from the weight of vengeance she had harbored, but it apparently left a burden on her heart instead. However, as she glanced at the pile of papers on Thanh's work desk, Mỹ Lệ realized that it was not the right time to share her feelings with a friend. She casually made a few jokes and gracefully withdrew.

Before parting ways, though, Mỹ Lệ asked for a bottle of iodine solution to keep at her house, using the excuse that her son had too many scratches and bruises lately. Thanh called a taxi to take Mỹ Lệ and Sáng home. Mỹ Lệ waved goodbye, saying "Adieu" with a half-smile. Thanh reached into the car to ruffle Sáng's hair and urged Thảo to say goodbye to Sáng.

As the taxi rolled away slowly, Thanh waved goodbye. Looking at Mỹ Lệ's weary face, she felt uneasy. After taking a few steps into the house, Thanh suddenly wondered why Mỹ Lệ had said "Adieu" in bidding farewell today. It sounded as if it were for an eternal separation. Thanh pondered, "Why didn't she say 'Au revoir,' the usual farewell like always?"

After dinner, as was their daily custom, Thanh and her 'daughter' would sit outside on the stone-inlay concrete bench in front of their house, relishing the evening breeze. Lý, their maid, joined them, taking a seat on the cement chest covering the water meter. Following the routine, Thanh enveloped Thảo in a warm hug, inquiring, "Whose mother is this?" Thảo responded, "This mother is my mother." Thanh posed another question, "Whose child is this?" Thảo confidently replied, "This child is your child." This daily exchange seemed to serve as a ritual, a reaffirmation of Thanh's involuntary role as a mother, a pledge to live in a manner that would assure her beloved sister in heaven, who had entrusted Thảo to her care.

Later, Thanh asked Thảo whether she enjoyed playing with Sáng earlier in the morning. Thảo responded straightforwardly, "No." Lý chimed in, saying, "Perhaps he's not accustomed to our surroundings. He wasn't as active as boys his age usually are." Thanh, recalling Mỹ Lệ's contrasting claim that Sáng had become quite mischievous and prone to accidents, found herself perplexed. The more she dwelled on it, the more confusion set in: "Why did Mỹ Lệ ask me for the bottle of disinfectant?" In a moment of realization, Thanh exclaimed, "Oh no," and promptly urged Lý to summon a nearby taxi driver. As Thanh waited in front of the house for the taxi, a jumble of emotions churned inside her.

Speculations continued to accumulate in Thanh's mind as she retreated into her thoughts on the backseat of the cab. The taxi eventually halted at the entrance of the alley, where the darkening sky hinted at the lateness of the hour. Thanh, determined, hurriedly traversed the distance to Mỹ Lệ's house and knocked on the door. Aunt Six, Mỹ Lệ's mother, opened it, and upon entering, Thanh immediately inquired about Mỹ Lệ.

"Both mother and child went to bed early today, and I don't know why," Aunt Six replied.

Growing more anxious, Thanh rushed into the inner room while calling Mỹ Lệ's name. Mỹ Lệ, in the midst of putting her child to sleep, responded with concern, "I'm here. What's the matter?"

Seating herself beside the bed, Thanh questioned her friend, "What are you doing?"

"I'm putting my child to sleep. I noticed he was a bit haggard today, so I decided to let him sleep a little earlier," Mỹ Lệ explained.

"Tell me the truth, why did you bring back the bottle of Teinture d'iode?" Thanh asked.

Mỹ Lệ hesitated and countered, "How did you know I was only using Sáng as an excuse to obtain the disinfectant?"

"I knew it. Come on, Mỹ Lệ. If there's anything you need, you could have just told me," Thanh replied.

"What are you saying?" Mỹ Lệ puzzled.

"Just imagine, if something happened to you, how would Sáng and Aunt Six cope?" Thanh explained.

"What? Do you think I want to take the disinfectant to kill myself?" Mỹ Lệ rushed to hug Thanh tightly, tears of happiness streaming down her face. Mỹ Lệ tried to express gratitude through an admiring smile, "I'm sorry, Thanh, for making you worry and have to rush here to save me at this time of the day. I appreciate you so much."

Mỹ Lệ held onto Thanh, gently stroking her back, and clarified, "The other day, my mom accidentally cut her hand, and we were running out of medicine at home. So, taking the opportunity to visit your place, I thought of getting a new supply."

"You're really mischievous. Why didn't you say that the medicine was for Aunt Six?" Thanh asked.

"To be honest, I was afraid it would make you sad, as it would remind you of your mom's tragic end," Mỹ Lệ said, alluding to Thanh's mother's death due to a minor cut in the finger. Mỹ Lệ tried to lighten the mood with a warm smile.

Now it was Thanh's turn to feel overwhelmed with emotion. She hugged Mỹ Lệ, reproaching her affectionately, "With all the troubles you have, you're still concerned about me, and afraid that I'll be upset. Really!"

Since the fateful day at the graveside of Thanh's mother until now, Thanh had always felt guilty for failing to protect her friend. Thanh hugged Mỹ Lệ tightly and whispered, "That day, I shouldn't have left you alone with that devil."

Mỹ Lệ quickly responded, "Are you still thinking about that? Forget it. That's in the past for me now."

"Really? I thought you carry a deep hatred for him," Thanh said.

"Listen to me, the reason I'd like to meet you this morning was just that. I wanted to tell you about that devil," Mỹ Lệ explained.

"Why didn't you say anything then?" Thanh asked.

"Partly because I saw you were busy. But you know me, I would rather keep things to myself. At home, I planned to tell you everything, but when I got there, I hesitated and didn't know what to say. Talking about myself seems awkward, so I stopped," Mỹ Lệ replied.

"Now, tell me the truth. Did you meet him?" Thanh asked.

Mỹ Lệ discreetly glanced into the front room to ensure her mother was asleep. Leaning in close to Thanh, she began recounting every detail of her encounter with Paul. Tears streamed down her face as she recalled the shocking moment when she recognized the familiar features of Sáng on his father's face. A pang of regret consumed her, blaming herself for denying her child the chance to meet his father.

Suddenly, a knock on the front door startled Aunt Six. "Who's there?" she mumbled, sitting up at the edge of the plank and searching for her wooden clogs. Dragging herself to the door, she announced, "There's a Frenchman at the door." Mỹ Lệ jolted, briefly considering the possibility that it might be Paul, but she dismissed the thought. Thanh, sensing her friend's confusion, hurried to the door. If Paul hadn't promptly introduced himself, Thanh wouldn't have recognized him; he no longer sported the scruffy beard from their last meeting at the gravesite. Thanh rushed back inside to inform Mỹ Lệ, who angrily responded, "Please go out there and chase him away for me."

Having shared their deepest thoughts and emotions, Thanh understood that Mỹ Lệ's tough exterior was a façade concealing profound pain. Sitting beside her friend, Thanh offered advice, "Look, you're back at it again. If something is bothering you, it's better to let it out. Keeping it inside will do you more harm than good."

Listening to her friend's reproachful yet loving admonishment, Mỹ Lệ reluctantly decided to meet Paul. She stood still, observing him humbly clad in a crisp white shirt. The innocent and pitiable look on Paul's face, reminiscent of Sáng caught in mischief, sought forgiveness from Mỹ Lệ, challenging her earlier determination. Reluctantly, she retreated to the table, sinking into her chair. Intentionally, Thanh invited Paul to sit next to Mỹ Lệ before discreetly withdrawing to the kitchen to prepare some tea. Aunt Six insisted on boiling the water herself, prompting Thanh to bid farewell, in the hope that Mỹ Lệ and Paul would find some privacy.

Mỹ Lệ quickly pleaded with Thanh to stay, "You're leaving me alone? Are you trying to kill me?" Her words, whether intentional or not, stirred Thanh's guilt for abandoning her friend the last time. Hesitating, Thanh pulled a chair to the edge of the table.

Paul felt momentarily awkward in the presence of the third party but considered it better than facing outright rejection from Mỹ Lệ. He looked at her and, in an almost whispered tone, hesitated before saying, "Thank you for meeting me. I know, no matter how many apologies I offer, it might be futile, but I still want to say it. Please forgive me."

Mỹ Lệ sat quietly, her eyes fixed on the table. Paul continued, "In fact, for the past two years after returning to Saigon, I've been trying to find you around the Xây Nho's Police Station, but no one knew where your family had moved to. Unfortunately, I had to meet you again in these circumstances. In any case, thanks to Năm Chảng, who not only helped me finally locate you but also shared with me what you went through."

Paul hesitated, stealing a brief glance towards Thanh. Thanh could discern a desire in him to express more of his feelings toward Mỹ Lệ, yet he seemed restrained in her presence. After a moment of silence, Paul noted that although Mỹ Lệ wasn't responding directly to him, her demeanor displayed less anger and distress than during their previous encounter. Encouraged by this subtle shift, he mustered the courage to unveil the purpose of his visit:

"May I request the opportunity to meet our son?"

Mỹ Lệ burst into tears. Tears streamed down, soaking the palms of her hands covering her face. The dreams of hearing Sáng call out "Dad" seemed futile for so long, but unexpectedly, they could become a reality right before her eyes. Thanh handed a handkerchief to Mỹ Lệ and gently rubbed her back to console her. Mỹ Lệ's unexpected reaction left Paul bewildered. He stood up, intending to comfort her, but remembering the slap from years ago made him hesitate. Thanh helped Mỹ Lệ stand up, speaking softly into her ear:

"Let them meet each other, my dear. Look, he's been holding a little box tightly in his hands all this time; probably a toy for the child. Have pity on him."

Seeing Mỹ Lệ not resisting, Thanh turned to invite Paul to join them inside the next room to meet Sáng. As soon as Paul had the glimpse of his sleeping child on the bed, he rushed to embrace him, kissing his forehead, nose, cheeks, and hair. Thanh quietly slipped away from behind the house, bidding farewell to Aunt Six. Suddenly, she felt a lightness, as if she had just shed a heavy burden that had been weighing on her for years. The woman's intuition signaled to Thanh that a wonderful happiness awaited her friend.

Thanh smiled dreamily, stepping towards the front of Mỹ Lệ's house, then turned back to say to Aunt Six:

"Please tell Mỹ Lệ later that my daughter is too mischievous nowadays; her grandmother is getting tired of looking after her. So, I have to go back and put her to bed. You just say it like that, and Mỹ Lệ will understand!"

Thanh smiled as she walked away, content after metaphorically 'returning the favor to Mỹ Lệ.' When Mỹ Lệ fabricated a tale about her son's mischievous antics at noon, Thanh now had her own excuse to gently distance herself. In the comfort of their shared private space, Thanh held onto the hope that sincere hearts would naturally gravitate towards one another. Silently, she prayed for the awaited dawn to finally break through, casting its light on the lives of her friend, her son, and even Paul - illuminating the path to happiness that lay ahead for each of them.

8. Nurse Thanh

Since Thảo turned four, Thanh's family relocated from the Bãi Sậy police compound to Cây Lý's Hamlet, settling into a house they purchased from an acquaintance. According to Thanh, the primary motivation behind this move was to prepare for Thảo's future. Feeling the need to integrate into the hamlet's community life, Thanh aimed to secure a job that would ensure a stable life for her family and support Thảo's education. Depending solely on her father's civil servant salary had become precarious due to the country's unstable situation and her father's declining health.

At present, Thảo is eight years old and attends the third grade with Teacher Mùi at Lý Thái Tổ Primary School, near the Bãi Sậy market. Following a family tradition initiated by Thanh, about a month before the school opening day, she would purchase fabric to sew three new sets of clothes for Thảo's upcoming school year. Two weeks before the school term commenced, Thanh would take Thảo to the bazaar outside the market to procure school supplies, encompassing notebooks, pencils, pens, ink, erasers, rulers, and more. Thảo would be well-equipped with everything she needed on the first day of school each year. Additionally, Thanh would purchase wrapping paper to cover all notebooks, along with labels to inscribe the student's name, class, school, and academic year.

Tonight, just three days before the school's opening day, Thanh meticulously arranged all the books, notebooks, and sheets of wrapping paper on the dining table at home. Thảo graciously assisted in covering the notebooks and books, while Thanh, seated at the adjacent table, dedicated herself to filling in the labels. With unwavering concentration on each calligraphic letter, she inscribed Thảo's name and the school's name with a calligraphic pen she always kept at home, accompanied by two ink bottles. The blue ink, usually reserved for writing wedding congratulatory notes, flowed smoothly as she crafted the labels for Thảo's notebooks.

Upon completing their respective tasks, the mother and daughter turned their attention to organizing Thảo's school bag. Thanh had a rule that prohibited toys from being kept in the bag, but Thảo had a fondness for playing with the fluffy, pristine white lining sheets inside injection medicine boxes. Aware that her mother prioritized education, Thảo requested permission to bring these lining sheets to school as blotting paper to prevent ink smudging in her notebooks. Thanh, seeing through her child's intentions, nevertheless readily offered an approving smile and quietly praised, 'She seems quite clever, and no less mischievous than I was at her age!'

Since the time Thanh felt comfortable letting Thảo go to school alone, without the need to accompany her every day as she did for almost two years before, she began to consider fulfilling her dream of finding a profession to support herself. In reality, she cared little for herself; her main concern was for her aging parents, and most importantly, for Thảo's future - how to ensure that her child would receive a good education and thrive.

Fortunately, there was an accelerated nursing course organized at Chợ Rẫy Hospital, and Thanh hurriedly enrolled. As of now, 'Nurse Thanh' has graduated and has been practicing administering injections for the local community for a few months.

During the time she was learning her profession, poor Thảo, every night after dinner, would often be brought out to play the role of a patient for Thanh's practical training. One night it might be a bandage on the hand, the next night on the forearm, and another night a bandage wrapped around the head. At least, after Thanh graduated and began practicing, Thảo also received a corresponding reward - keeping some soft, pristine white papers found inside a few French medicine boxes to play with.

As part of Thanh's newfound career, every day after dinner, she would ride her bike into the alleys behind her house to visit patients. Usually, when she went out, she brought Thảo along to avoid unwanted attention from young men. However, when going to the homes of patients for injections, she didn't bring her daughter along, fearing exposure to infectious cases.

Today, Thanh went to Uncle Tám's, the mason's, house. After years of hard work, Uncle Tám had managed to save up a bit to build a house with brick walls and a tin roof - an upscale dwelling in a place where most houses were made of mud walls and roofing covered by dried coconut leaves. However, since his tuberculosis worsened, he no longer had the breath to perform strenuous mason work, and the family had fallen into hardship. When his mother was alive, she helped babysit his children at home so his wife could peddle food on the street to earn a little extra money to buy rice. Unfortunately, a few months ago, his mother passed away suddenly. Now, his wife, Aunt Tám, turned to the job of making food bags for a grocery store. From noon until evening, Aunt Tám and her three children would gather to make paper bags on the ground in front of their house. Each bag earned them 2 cents.

Since early morning, Sóc, the 12-year-old eldest son of Aunt Tám, had been wearing a stack of empty cement bags on his head, carrying them to the riverbank to shake off dust. Typically, he had to stand under the scorching sun until noon, raising a cement bag high, letting it float in front of him, while using a stick to beat the bag until it was visually clear of dust. In the process, fine cement dust flew in all directions, scattering in the wind like misty smoke, and before long, white cement powder covered his hair, ears, face, and bare chest. The external dust could be washed away by jumping into the river, but what about the harm caused by the cement accumulating daily inside his two young lungs? It seemed like no one wanted to know, except for Thanh, who often shared her concerns with Thảo.

Thanh had just parked her bike in front of Uncle Tám's house when she heard Aunt Tám's voice.

"Dear Miss Thanh, how are you?" Aunt Tám greeted.

"Welcome, Miss Thanh," echoed the voices of Aunt Tám's children. They were sitting on the dirt, circling around piles of cut-up papers retrieved from cement bags.

Aunt Tám instructed her son, "Sóc, go pour some water to offer Miss Thanh."

"It's alright, Aunt Tám. I've had my meal before coming here," Thanh said, touching Sóc on the shoulder, signaling that he didn't have to stand up.

"How is Uncle Tám doing? Is he feeling better nowadays?" Thanh asked, her inquiry echoing more like a prayer than a casual question, knowing the fate of a patient entering the final stage of this debilitating disease.

"You know, I didn't dare to come and invite you lately. The money we earned is not enough to eat, let alone buy medicine for him. We can't keep bothering you for the medicine all the time; it's not right. My husband is also reluctant to trouble you, so he said, 'Let things be as they may,'" Aunt Tám explained.

"Well, sickness is nobody's fault. Uncle Tám shouldn't worry about troubling me. I'll do what I can. Today, I received some bottles of sample medicines from the pharmacist, so I brought them to administer to Uncle Tám," Thanh replied.

"My family and I are really grateful to you. Not only for the medicine but also for your kindness. We truly don't know how to repay you," Aunt Tám expressed her gratitude.

Thanh stepped around to where Aunt Tám's daughter, Mận, was sitting. Mận is the same age as Thảo but, due to family circumstances, couldn't go to school. She sat beside the cracked bowl of paste in the dim light of a flickering oil lamp nearby on the ground. Holding a piece of dried coconut shell, Mận dipped it into the bowl and then spread the paste onto the edge of each square sheet of paper. Her brother folded and sealed it to make a paper bag. Mận's slender arms repeated the skilled, monotonous motions, resembling the drawing of a dead-end alley in the darkness of the night.

Thanh sighed wearily as she entered the house, ready to administer the medicine to Uncle Tám. On her way back home, she struggled to pedal her bike, burdened by a sinking heart and a melancholic sadness. She felt powerless in the face of the tragedies surrounding her, sympathizing with those in need but lacking the ability to alleviate the heart-wrenching situations unfolding before her.

Even the medicine samples she obtained from the pharmacists, which other nurses could sell for extra income, were used by Thanh to provide free injections for her patients. In some cases, such as with another patient, Mr. Năm, a few months ago, she dipped into her own pocket to buy medicine for him. Mr. Năm's eyes were severely infected, turning red with inflammation, and his eyelids were swollen. Thanh, fearing he might go blind if left untreated, purchased vials of antibiotic medicine to administer regularly to him.

Thanh pondered how much she could truly help people like Mr. Năm and Uncle Tám, especially given the precarious situation her family was in. The deteriorating health of her father added to her constant worries. She often wondered about the potential repercussions if her father were to face early retirement or, worse, get laid off, as the family's livelihood would then squarely rest on her shoulders.

9. A Magical Event

This morning, as Thanh sat down for breakfast, she noticed unease in her father. Restlessness emanated from him, his gaze repeatedly shifting towards the dishwashing area in the backyard, with a palpable worry lingering in his distant eyes. Concern washed over Thanh as she sensed her father's troubled mood. Despite the urge to inquire, she hesitated, grappling with uncertainty about what to say and a fear of inadvertently provoking his anger. Their family, even in the best of times, seldom engaged in sharing feelings.

When Thanh returned from the market, her father hurriedly intercepted her before she could carry the groceries to the kitchen. He pointed towards the large 250-gallon clay jar, which stored fresh water reserved for family cooking, and instructed Thanh, "Go tell the servant to dump all the water from that jar out."

"Why, Dad?" Thanh asked in confusion. "If we dump that water, what will we use for cooking our rice?"

"Tell the maid to fetch fresh water from the rainwater barrels in the back of the house," replied her father.

"Is this water contaminated or something, Dad?"

"Last night, I saw Mạnh sneak into our house and pour a basin of blood into that jar."

Mạnh, the police officer, replaced Mr. Tư on patrol duty at the local market. However, after a brief period of Mạnh overseeing the market, he faced reprimand for extorting vendors. He falsely accused Mr. Tư of informing the authorities about his misconduct.

"Why would Officer Mạnh do something like that, Dad?" Thanh inquired.

"Earlier, I had a run-in with him, and he holds a grudge, aiming to frame me with some fabricated trouble," her father explained.

Thanh quickly ran over, opened the lid of the water jar, and took a peek inside. Startled, she asked, "I still see clear water, Dad."

"I asked you to empty that jar; just do it," her father insisted.

Thanh reached for the aluminum can hanging nearby, intending to scoop up some water to double-check. This infuriated her father, and he shouted loudly, "Don't touch it. Stay away. If you guys don't do it, I'll do it."

Upon his sudden outburst, Thanh quickly raised her hand in surrender, saying, "Alright, Dad, let me call Lý to change the water."

Mr. Tư, with a sense of hesitation, walked through the house's corridor, passing the row of paperbark trees by the edge of the fish pond. After a moment of contemplation, he hesitated before grabbing the bicycle parked by the side of the house and pedaling out of the gate in a state of dejection.

A few days later, in the early morning, amid the lively chirping of sparrows weaving through the branches among the lush leaves of the rows of paperbark trees that Mr. Tư had planted alongside the pond when the family first moved here, Thanh stood by the water basin, ready to perform her daily ritual of brushing her teeth and washing her face. Though not fully awake, she sensed an unusual presence - her father standing nearby, his gaze fixed intently on the top of one of the slim, tall trees without uttering a word.

Wiping her face, Thanh inquired, "What are you doing, Dad?"

Mr. Tư remained silent, taking a step closer to Thanh, his eyes still locked on the tree's apex. He whispered his command, "Go see the handyman 'Bảy', and ask him to cut down all these trees."

Puzzled, Thanh furrowed her brows, concerned about her father's recent peculiar behavior. This row of trees was nurtured by him, with eager anticipation for the day it would cast shade along the corridor beside the house.

The front door of Thanh's house seldom saw use; family members and visitors alike walked straight from the corridor to the side door, sheltered by the paperbark trees. Mr. Tư would daily set up a reclining chair on the walkway, engrossed in reading the newspaper or contemplating poetry. Passersby, if inclined, would be familiar with Cung Oán Ngâm Khúc or Chinh Phụ Ngâm, the Vietnamese classic poems he recited loudly each day. If not reading poetry, he would engage in a game of chess. The chessboard, always prepared for battle, rested on a small table between the two middle trees.

These trees had become integral to his daily world. So, why the sudden decision to cut them down? Moreover, every evening he eagerly awaited the return of the sparrow flock to their nests, relishing the lively chirping on the branches. While some in the house disliked the early morning bird chorus, Mr. Tư found joy in waking up to their cheerful melody. The more Thanh pondered it, the more perplexed she became.

Mr. Tư, upon returning from his coffee break, inquired, "Why haven't you cut down the trees yet?"

Attempting to subtly dissuade her father, Thanh responded, "I thought you enjoyed bringing the reclining chair under this row of paperbark trees to read the newspaper in the afternoon?"

"From now on, I'll sit in the hallway in front of the house. It's quieter there."

"What are you talking about? You never liked sitting right in front of our house, facing passers-by on the street. There's more privacy on the side of the house, and there's also a cool spot for you to play chess."

Mr. Tư didn't reply; he bowed his head sadly. Ignoring Thanh, he let his gaze wander toward the top of a tree, his distant eyes conveying thoughts to a faraway place. Then, he silently entered the house. The next morning, as Thanh brushed her teeth, he approached and whispered, "Today, you must cut down this row of trees."

"I thought you had changed your mind."

"Last night, I saw them gathering again."

"Who are you talking about?"

"Those guys killed by the police. They gathered here, planning revenge."

"Where did you see them?"

"They're hiding on the top of these trees."

Feeling a sense of dread, Thanh asked, for the sake of asking,

"The tree branches are so tiny; how can they hide up there?"

A profound sadness overwhelmed Thanh; she had no more doubts. Her father's mental state had deteriorated drastically. There was no time to wait; she had to act now - finding immediate treatment for him. But... how to convince someone who could no longer distinguish between reality and illusion that they were living in a world that is not real? And how to handle the stigma associated with mental illness in society? Numerous unanswered questions besieged her. Exhausted, Thanh slumped into the chair beside the dining table.

Mrs. Tư returned from the market, and before she could put the basket down, little Thảo clung to her, asking if Grandma had bought rice cakes for her to eat. The scene was so familiar on other days, but today it stirred worries in Thanh. She wondered how the family's situation would turn out if her father were suddenly fired from his job. Being a civil servant, he normally could rely on a pension and 'Rappel' (retirement and pension benefits) to maintain a stable life in old age. But what if he were fired or forced to retire early? Thanh was troubled by negative thoughts when a maid, the one who cleaned and rolled up the mat on Mr. Tư's bed every morning, hurriedly approached and whispered in her ear: "Miss Thanh, why does Mr. Tư have a machete under his pillow?"

Thanh's face turned pale. The situation was becoming more critical than she had thought. Thanh began to worry about the safety of the household members. She quietly advised the maid: "From now on, every night before going to bed, remember to hide all the knives in the kitchen."

"Where should I hide them?"

"After washing the dishes each night, gather all the knives and place them in a basket, then hide them under your bed. Only take them out to use the next morning."

Thanh then approached her father for an investigation, "This morning, the maid found a machete on your bed. Did you whittle the fishing rod yesterday and forget it there, Dad?"

Mr. Tư, lost in a distant gaze, murmured to himself, "Tonight, they'll come back, and I'll kill them all."

"Who, Dad?" Thanh hesitated to ask, but in her heart, she already knew the answer. They were just imaginary enemies in her father's troubled mind. Mr. Tư turned away and walked off, as if he hadn't heard the question or didn't want to answer.

Throughout the night, Thanh remained vigilant, tirelessly searching for a solution to aid her father. In the neighborhood of Cây Lý, where her family had recently relocated, familiar faces were scarce, and finding trustworthy individuals to offer assistance proved challenging. Thanh contemplated reaching out to her father's old acquaintances, but since his relocation to this remote outpost, opportunities to reconnect had been rare. Although her father's colleagues in the vicinity were casual friends, Thanh wondered whom she could genuinely rely on. Ultimately, she chose to keep the matter a closely guarded secret from them and sought support from her father's former colleagues at the Xây-nho police station.

Thanh quickly thought of Mỹ Lệ. Even though she had relocated from the police compound after her father's passing, she continued to stay in touch with some old acquaintances. The following morning, Thanh braved a nearly six-kilometer bike ride under the scorching sun to reach her friend's house.

After Thanh shared the entire situation, Mỹ Lệ fell into silent contemplation, brainstorming ways to assist. Suddenly, she asked, "Do you still remember Uncle Năm Hoan and Uncle Tư Cồn?"

"Yes, I remember them. Those young uncles used to drink with our dads."

"Yeah, we call them 'uncle' because they're friends of our fathers. Actually, they're not much older than us. They started working early, just right after they finished Brevet (First Level Secondary School Certificate)."

"I know. They were just four grades above us... But, why did you bring them up?"

"I heard they got promoted quickly because they were trained and developed through the French system. Unlike our fathers who could go so far in their career, because they spoke only broken French."

"Where are they now?" Thanh eagerly asked.

"These two uncles now work at the Central Police Station. Uncle Năm Hoan seems to be the head of the personnel department, and as for Uncle Tư Cổn, I'm not sure; he seems to be involved with the 'secret police' unit. I wonder if they can be of any help."

"Thanks, at least they know my dad. Let me check them out."

Thanh parted ways with Mỹ Lệ without any specific plan. These two 'uncles' weren't close family friends whom she could ask for advice on her father's situation. However, to avoid letting people at the Bãi Sậy police station know, fearing the impact on her father's job, Thanh thought she should at least meet Uncle Năm Hoan first. He worked in the personnel department, so he might be able to offer a solution, she thought. As for Uncle Tư Cổn, who worked in the 'secret police' unit, the mere thought of it sent shivers down Thanh's spine. The next day, Thanh rode her bike to the Central Police Station, intending to find Uncle Năm Hoan. However, he was away on a business trip. Thanh had no choice but to find her way to visit Uncle Tư Cổn. As the daughter of a police officer, she had no problem finding someone who could direct her to Tư Cổn's office.

Standing nervously outside the office door, Thanh initiated the conversation:

"Excuse me, Uncle Tư, I am the daughter of Mr. Tư formely from the Xây-nho's police station."

Tư Cổn, after a moment of squinting, recognized Thanh. He used to notice 'little Thanh' since the day he came to her house to have occasional drinks with her father and eagerly seized the opportunity.

"Oh, you're Thanh, right? My, just call me 'brother.' It sounds better."

Tư Cổn wrapped his arm around Thanh's shoulder, guiding her to a guest chair, then pulled his chair to sit across from her. He chuckled, showing all of his teeth, and asked, 'Did you come to visit me?'

"Yes, I had the chance to return to the Xây-nho station to visit Mỹ Lệ, Uncle Sáu's daughter, and I heard from her that you work here."

"Don't call me 'uncle,' call me 'brother,'" Tư Cổn insisted.

Since entering his office, Thanh had already endured Tư Cổn's unwarranted shoulder hug, and now she had to tolerate his inappropriate words. His demeanor and language offended her deeply, but she endeavored to remain composed while seeking assistance for her father. Yet, her instincts warned her that someone like him thrived on exploiting others rather than offering genuine help. Furthermore, noting his current job title as displayed on his desk, Deputy Chief of the Central Bureau of Intelligence, Thanh felt an even stronger urge to maintain a safe distance. 'Predators like him will seize any sign of weakness,' she thought, swiftly avoiding divulging the real reason for her visit.

"My father is approaching retirement age, so I wanted to inquire about pension matters from Uncle Năm Hoan. Unfortunately, he's on a business trip today, so I took the opportunity to visit you."

Tư Cổn slyly placed his hand on Thanh's thigh.

"That's great! Let me take you to Brodard for ice cream, and then we can chat more."

Thanh promptly stood up, taking a step toward the door, suppressing the indignation in her heart to respond calmly, "Thank you, but I have to go home. My father is waiting." Tư Cổn was taken aback by Thanh's determined attitude. Before he could resort to other tactics, Thanh had already reached the door. He looked after her with regret. Instinctively, he briefly considered using force, but the thought of Năm Hoan and the connection with Thanh's father made him refrain from any violent action. He could only sit there, regretting and watching his prey slip away.

On the way back home, Thanh reproached herself for not being as cautious as she should have been, lowering her head against the rain and pedaling her bike as fast as her small legs allowed. It was a visible attempt to channel her anger into battling the elements. Even the heavens seemed to agree, unleashing a downpour like a waterfall. Undeterred, Thanh persisted in challenging the forces of nature. Grinding her teeth under her palm-leaf conical hat, which shielded her from complete soaking, Thanh pedaled recklessly, flying through the wind, cutting through the rain. Approaching an intersection simultaneously with a white Peugeot, she was fortunate to encounter a slow-moving vehicle, avoiding a direct collision. However, the bike's rear was lightly brushed, causing Thanh to fall onto the wet pavement, with her limbs scraped.

Trường, a young owner of the car sitting in the back, hurried to help Thanh up, unexpectedly facing her fierce reaction. As Trường knelt behind Thanh, she shouted, "Get away!" and swung her arm, knocking him onto the road. His once bright white suit was now soaked with rainwater and mud. Surprisingly, Trường didn't get angry but was captivated by Thanh's radiant face, her eyes expressing more determination and sensitivity than anger or hatred.

Trường tried to express concern, but with a more cautious attitude:

"Please allow me to take you to the hospital."

Awkwardly standing up, feeling a sharp pain in her knee, Thanh collapsed into Trường's waiting arms. Trường guided Thanh to sit at the back of the car, instructing the driver to take her to Grall, a high-end hospital built for French citizens during the colonial years.

Trường's warm voice and caring demeanor made Thanh feel safer. "What about my bike?" Thanh reminded.

"Don't worry, the bike is in the trunk; the driver will take it for repairs later."

"Thank you," Thanh said, touching her knee apologetically, "I'm sorry for being impolite earlier." Hearing Thanh suddenly soften her tone and address him as '*anh*' (older brother), Trường smiled and introduced himself:

"I'm Trường. May I know your name?"

"Yes, my name is Thanh."

A moment of silence enveloped them, each person lost in their own thoughts. Thanh began to feel uneasy sharing a ride with a stranger. A comparison between Trường and 'Uncle Tư Cổn' suddenly occurred to her. One side had made Thanh cautious from the very moment of their greeting, while the other had the potential to dismantle Thanh's defensive instincts.

Trường broke the silence, expressing his regret, "I'm sorry, Thanh. The driver tried his best but couldn't avoid it, leaving you in this situation."

"No, it's my fault for rushing headlong without paying attention to the road."

"As long as you're safe, that's what matters. Do you feel better now?"

Thanh rubbed her injured knee, tried to stretch her leg, then nodded and said, "The knee doesn't hurt anymore. Maybe you can just fix the bike, and I can ride it home."

Trường advised Thanh to let the nurse take care of the scratches on her hands and arms to avoid infection. Although Thanh was haunted by the risk of Tetanus infection (causing lockjaw) that led to the death of her biological mother, her greater concern was that if something happened to her, there would be no one to take care of her elderly parents and the daughter of her late sister.

Thanh hesitated but eventually agreed to accompany Trường to the hospital. She whispered anxiously:

"I hope the doctor will examine me quickly; my father is waiting at home."

Trường reassured her, "I'll take you back. Where do you live?"

"Near Bãi Sậy Police Station, but I wouldn't want to trouble you."

"Oh, that far? And you pedaled your bike all the way here? Don't worry; I'll take you home. I'd like to visit your part of town anyway."

"It's a suburban area, half rural, half urban. There's not much to see."

"Actually, I've been away from Vietnam for six years and just returned a few weeks ago. While away, I missed it a lot, and upon my return, I felt restless, wanting to revisit the familiar places. As for new places like Bãi Sậy District, I haven't had the chance to visit it before; I would really like to explore it now."

"Apparently, you went abroad for studying, so are you an engineer or a doctor?"

"Yes, I did study in France, but why do you assume my profession could be as such?"

"Well, I've heard that wealthy people send their children to study in France hoping they will become engineers or doctors. Of course, there are also those who, after being away from home, become carefree, abandon their studies, and bring back a foreign wife."

"Why didn't you consider me part of the third category then?"

Thanh looked embarrassed, glancing through the glass window. The raindrops had become sparse. Trường intended not to delve further into his personal life, as he was unsure about the future, but found Thanh's comments intriguing. Hesitatingly, he said:

"In addition, there is a fourth category you didn't mention."

Thanh responded, "I just casually made a general remark; I don't know anything about those categories."

"Back in France, I befriended an older fellow who had graduated as an engineer. After returning home, I visited him, and... you know what he is doing now."

"Probably working for the government or teaching, right?"

Trường nodded again, appreciating Thanh's response.

"You know, you always have interesting observations, or at least thoughts that make people ponder."

"If you think I sound rustic, just say it; I don't know much about your world."

"But, I genuinely think so. Your observations indicate that in our society, people study to either pursue positions in government or become educators. And that's just what it was throughout our history. People would try to pass a national exam to be a mandarin; if that didn't work out, they'd return home to be a teacher, still commanding some respect from society. Today is no different. Students studying abroad return home with a degree, regardless of their field of specialty, just to aim for positions like deputy director or department head in the government. Otherwise, they follow the teaching path to become professors, which is also held in high esteem. It's a cycle of one generation teaching the next, without ever applying what they know for any practical applications that could help develop the country."

"So, is your friend in a government position or teaching?"

"No, he manages the family's coal and rice depot. Unfortunately, he often endures public mockery, being called the 'Engineer who sells coal.'"

"It seems like a waste of education, doesn't it?"

"Indeed, he couldn't apply his technical learning effectively. However, he might be contributing to society in a vital way, fostering the development of commerce and industry, aligned with the principles of the Duy Tân Reform Movement."

"National affairs can be overwhelming for me; I struggle to manage my own home. But you've sparked my curiosity; I'm interested in knowing the path you've chosen in serving the country."

"Currently, I don't fit into any of the categories you mentioned, and the future is uncertain." Trường hesitated, reluctant to divulge too much about his personal life, but he continued: "I studied engineering and have graduated, but I hesitate to call myself an engineer because I've never practiced the profession, except for a brief period as an intern at a French water pump manufacturer."

"You're too modest. I know of a friend of an uncle who falls into the third category, marrying a French wife and claiming to be an engineer. However, according to his colleagues, he only graduated as a technician."

Trường smiled, contemplating the destiny of his country, where the radiance of science and technology had yet to reach every corner. Armed with a degree in Agricultural Engineering, he resisted his father's efforts to secure him a directorial position at the Ministry of Economy through influential connections. Opting for a career in agriculture, he was propelled by a deep-seated commitment to contribute to the advancement of farming in his nation, steadfastly rejecting the trappings of a bureaucratic regime.

Since his youth, Trường had admired the reformist ideas of the patriotic scholar Phan Châu Trinh. These ideas were influenced, in part, by Phan's observations of the transformative role played by Japanese entrepreneurs in their nation-building endeavors. Phan Châu Trinh actively championed the Duy Tân Reform Movement, advocating for the modernization of his homeland with a focus on 'developing people's intellect, uplifting people's spirit, and improving people's lives.' In Trường's interpretation, the latter emphasized the advancement of commerce as a means to facilitate prosperity among the populace.

"We've reached our destination, and the rain has finally ceased," Thanh's voice interrupted Trường's reflections.

The car came to a stop under a canopy of tamarind trees. Trường attentively guided Thanh to the medical examination room, observing each careful step she took on the damp asphalt. Above them, fresh green tamarind leaves, still glistening with raindrops, gracefully allowed a few sunbeams to playfully dance on Thanh's shoulders and the hair of the two wanderers.

After leaving the hospital, Trường suggested taking Thanh home, but she declined, wishing to avoid arousing more suspicion from her father about the reasons for being away from home all day. Besides, she was also reluctant to have Trường meet her father in his current state of mind.

While cycling home, an unbidden smile graced Thanh's face. Memories of her engaging conversations with Trường flooded her mind, vividly portraying his free-spirited charm as a refined gentleman. She replayed the touching yet slightly awkward moments when she felt his caring attention. Their brief, unexpected encounter amid the pouring rain felt like a magical event, leaving the sky aglow with warmth in Thanh's heart.

As she pedaled along, attempting to elongate the joyous moments with each revolution of the bike wheels, groundless worries began to insidiously seep into her soul. These unfounded concerns cast threatening clouds on the horizon, representing an accumulation of persistent unrest that had shadowed Thanh throughout her formative years.

Upon arriving home, Thanh was met with her father's distant and mysterious gaze, again casting a shadow over the flickering rays of spring in her heart, replaced by the swirling dark clouds of reality. That night, in the encompassing darkness, Thanh lay awake, contemplating whether to return to the 'Central' Police Station the next day to seek out Uncle Năm Hoan. Despite the fear instilled by her encounter with Tư Cổn earlier, Thanh's woman's intuition offered a sense of reassurance regarding Năm Hoan. Despite her optimistic thoughts, finding comfort and courage through self-convincing proved to be a struggle as she yearned for a peaceful night's sleep.

Fortunately, as Thanh had anticipated, Năm Hoan harbored fond memories of the good old days shared with Mr. Tư and was willing to extend a helping hand. He personally drove the department's Jeep to Thanh's house, feigning an invitation for Mr. Tư to join him for a drink. However, Năm Hoan had a different agenda; he headed straight to Chợ Quán Hospital and urgently advised Mr. Tư to be admitted for treatment. After numerous persuasions, Mr. Tư reluctantly agreed to undergo the "electric shock" treatment, involving the passage of a hundred volts through his temples.

From that point onward, Thanh dedicated herself to visiting and caring for her father daily. Aware that the "electric shock" treatment induced a "feverish" feeling, Thanh concocted watercress and lettuce soup to "cool down the temperature." Understanding that this procedure could weaken patients, she diligently prepared dishes rich in meat and eggs to provide nourishment for her father. The journey to the hospital involved crossing three imposing iron bridges, a challenge even for young men on bikes. Undeterred, every noon, carrying a basket of rice and chicken, Thanh persisted in cycling up those daunting bridge slopes to deliver food to her father.

No external force compelled her to endure the painstaking effort of pedaling up those stiff slopes; she could have walked her bike to the top of the bridge instead. However, she chose to undertake the challenge as an expression of gratitude to the divine, the Buddha, and her ancestors. Thanh fervently hoped that their watchful eyes would protect her father and aid in his swift recovery from the harrowing ordeal.

10. Familial Duty

From the late months of 1954, following the Geneva Accords, France withdrew its troops to the south of the 17th parallel, and by April 1956, had permanently withdrawn from Vietnam. This period witnessed the division of the country into North and South, guided by their divergent ideological inclinations. The South experienced a political upheaval, culminating in the Referendum of 1955, which ousted the last monarch of the country. The overthrow of the feudal era marked the beginning of a new epoch with the establishment of the Republic of Vietnam in the southern half of the country.

The South Vietnamese government initially grappled with unrest caused by remnants of paramilitary groups. Among the insurgent factions persisting from the colonial French regime, the Bình Xuyên paramilitary force rose prominently. Exerting substantial influence over the Saigon-Cholon metropolitan area, they controlled ports, bus stations, numerous entertainment venues, and internationally renowned gambling establishments such as Kim Chung and Đai Thế Giới casinos.

The Bình Xuyên forces had previously formed alliances with both the French and, at different junctures, with the Việt Minh - a Vietnamese organization striving for independence from the French - depending on the shifting dynamics of the conflict to mutually exploit advantages.

Bình Xuyên later formed a coalition with units from the armed forces of the Cao Đài and Hòa Hảo religious sects, exerting pressure on the government to secure broader participation in the new cabinet of Prime Minister Ngô Đình Diệm. Following the government's rejection of this coalition's demands, Bình Xuyên forces initiated military actions, launching attacks on the National Defence Headquarters and the Governor General's Palace, later known as the Independence Palace - the central seat of power for the Republic of Vietnam government.

The city of Saigon boasted a natural security buffer to the south - the Tẻ Canal, originating from the Saigon River, stretching over four kilometers from east to west before merging with the Bến Nghé Canal to form the Đôi Canal. This waterway continued its course southwest toward the Mekong Delta. The Bình Xuyên forces were scattered on both sides of these major canals, spanning from the Khánh Hội area in the east to the Rạch Cát area in the west. However, in a swift three-day operation, the main forces of the National Army's Paratroopers expelled the Bình Xuyên from the metropolitan area, seizing a critical Bình Xuyên position near Chánh Hưng's pig slaughterhouse.

The majority of the Bình Xuyên forces were compelled to retreat to their concealed hideout in the forest of Rừng Sát, while some scattered units remained covertly stationed on both sides of the major southern canals, biding their time for a new opportunity. Four months later, Prime Minister Ngô Đình Diệm assigned Colonel Dương Văn Minh of the Army of the Republic of Vietnam to launch Operation Hoàng Diệu, sustaining the pursuit of the Bình Xuyên rebels.

The precarious and unstable situation in South Vietnam cast a shadow of uncertainty. If the pro-American government were to prevail and bring stability, the established positions of old French-aligned factions, including Trường's family, might face upheaval. Confronted with this uncertain future, Trường made the decision to leave the country and establish himself in Cambodia. His paternal uncle, who had owned a hotel in Phnom Penh for many years, provided a promising connection.

Additionally, Trường has maintained a friendly relationship with the country's prince, Prince Norodom Sihanouk, forged during their shared time at Collège Chasseloup-Laubat in Saigon. Trường holds the belief that the Prince, with an honorary status as a reserve officer in the French army and having undergone training at the renowned Saumur Cavalry School in France, would be inclined to align his country with France rather than the United States.

While Trường was in the midst of packing for his journey to Phnom Penh, he coincidentally caught wind of the unfolding conflict through a radio broadcast in the adjacent room. The Bình Xuyên forces had retreated to the Bình An area near the Cây Lý neighborhood, and government forces were gearing up to pursue them that very night.

Concerned for Thanh's safety, Trường swiftly made his way to the Cây Lý hamlet to relay the urgent news. Hailing from the First District, his vehicle navigated Trần Hưng Đạo Boulevard. However, progress came to a halt after passing the Central Police Station, as the road was obstructed due to intense clashes between government forces and the steadfast supporters of Bình Xuyên. They had chosen to stay behind and defend the Đại Thế Giới casino in Cholon.

Determined to reach Thanh while avoiding the sealed-off combat zone, Trường abandoned his car on the side of the road and sprinted south. Winding through narrow alleys, he was taken aback to find that the smaller streets were bustling with activity, in stark contrast to the desolate boulevard and shuttered storefronts on the main thoroughfares. Seeking guidance to Tàu Hủ canal, where he could access the waterways leading to Thanh's vicinity, Trường asked locals for directions.

Upon arriving at the canal, Trường discovered an unusual calm. Families that typically anchored their boats along the waterway had been relocated for several days to evade potential danger. Fortunately, his path intersected with a father and son who owned a fishing boat. Through adept negotiation, Trường secured passage on their smaller vessel, albeit at a substantial cost, allowing him to reach the Cây Lý hamlet and deliver the crucial information to Thanh.

As the boat gently glided into the An Thông Hạ Canal, approaching the Distillery Bridge, Trường observed clusters of people hurriedly traversing the bridge, evacuating the Cây Lý hamlet in a steady stream. Adults and children alike gathered on the grassy expanse outside the wall of the French Distillery. Trường initially speculated that they believed they had distanced themselves enough from the war zone, opting to halt and seek refuge by the wall. Lacking the luxury of time to ascertain the true reason, he hastened his pace towards Thanh's house.

Thanh's family, uncertain about where to find shelter, considered returning to the police housing area at the Xây-Nho's police compound, hoping to encounter familiar faces who could offer temporary accommodation overnight. However, Trường relayed the grim news that all major routes had been blocked, making it nearly impossible to reach their intended destination.

Curious about the multitude seeking refuge outside the liquor factory wall, Trường discovered that they believed it to be a safer haven, convinced that the Bình Xuyên would refrain from attacking the French-owned liquor facility. Rumors suggested that the Bình Xuyên received support from the French, leveraging their influence in the struggle against Premier Ngô Đình Diệm's regime, particularly in competition with the United States.

A realization dawned on Trường. Having previous connections with the Chief Accountant of the liquor factory through banking services, he proposed to Thanh's family that they follow him to seek temporary shelter in the chief accountant's apartment within the distillery compound, ensuring an even safer refuge.

The entire family unanimously agreed to seek refuge, with the exception of Mr. Tư, who staunchly insisted on staying behind to guard the house. Using the rationale that he was accustomed to the sounds of bullets and bombs, Mr. Tư remained determined to hold his ground. Thanh assumed the responsibility of leading her mother and little Thảo, following Trường towards safety.

Crossing the Distillery Bridge, they reached the two iron gates typically guarded by a towering and heavily bearded Sikh soldier, his face obscured below the eyes by a black turban. These Sikh individuals of Indian origin, renowned for their bravery in the British colonial army, were often recruited by French companies in Vietnam to serve as "gardiens" (gatekeepers) safeguarding French-owned interests. In anticipation of potential disturbances, the factory had deployed four Sikh guards armed with rifles to stand watch at the gate.

Approaching the factory gate, Trường sought permission to meet with Mr. Beausoleil. A Sikh guard entered the post and made a phone call. After a brief wait, Mr. Beausoleil emerged to greet Trường at the gate. His family resided in an elegant row-house within the factory compound, and the two conversed in French. Mr. Beausoleil informed Trường that they were welcome to stay overnight, but there were only two available beds - sufficient for three people in Thanh's family. As a result,

Trường resigned himself to sleeping on a camp bed arranged on the front porch.

After everyone had retired for the night, Trường and Thanh remained seated on the front porch, sharing their thoughts in the quietude. The earlier echoes of cannon fires, which had continuously reverberated from the dark horizon, had now ceased. The fiery streaks of bullets that once tore through the sky had vanished, making room for the twinkling stars patiently waiting in the night shadows. In this moment of serenity, Trường patiently awaited Thanh's response, having previously hinted at marriage twice and encountered her silent reservation.

Despite cherishing their friendship, Thanh had never allowed herself to break free from the constraints of duty to her family, which she imposed upon herself. However, on this particular night, Trường seized the opportunity to seek clarity from her before departing Vietnam.

"The state of the country is still so chaotic, don't you think?" Trường inquired.

"Yes, when do you think things will get better?" Thanh responded.

"If I knew the answer, I wouldn't have decided to leave the country. The United States, being a superpower that survived World War II, might be able to help the government and eventually suppress rebels like the Bình Xuyên. But the question remains: What happens next? What will be the outcome of the upcoming general election between the North and the South? Who will emerge victorious, and who will face defeat? And, crucially, whether the losing side adheres to democratic principles and lays down their weapons after the election?"

"The situation is indeed too complicated, isn't it? I don't want us to find ourselves fleeing to the countryside once again to seek refuge from the war."

Trường, understanding the gravity of Thanh's concerns, offered a tactful solution, "Then let my parents come and ask your father for our marriage. After that, we can take your parents and little Thảo to live peacefully in Phnom Penh."

This proposal aimed at safeguarding Thanh's entire family, acknowledging the paramount importance she placed on her familial commitments. Despite Trường's assurance and capability to fulfill his promise, Thanh found herself unable to accept his offer. Memories of the farewell party at Trường's house flashed through her mind. On that occasion, intentional or not, Trường had revealed two suitcases filled with stacks of hundred piaster bills, alongside mentioning his family's widespread investments in the import and export of farm equipment and agricultural products in Phnom Penh, Cambodia.

Suddenly, Trường startled Thanh with his earnest inquiry, "What do you think?"

Moved by the realization of Trường's sacrifices and his consistent efforts to aid her and her family during challenging times, even at the risk of his own life, Thanh expressed her deep emotions, "You know, it touched me so much, the thought that you've sacrificed a lot to help me and my family in difficult times, even when it could endanger your life, like this time. And I really haven't been able to do anything in return..."

Trường interrupted, "This is the biggest obstacle. You're too rational. What I hope for is for you to question yourself: Do you love me? I'm just waiting for that. I'm waiting for the answer from your heart. I never thought of myself as a loan shark demanding repayment."

"I'm sorry. I truly apologize. I misspoke. Although my words were sincere, they may have come out the wrong way," Thanh responded.

Trường, softening his stance, "Actually, the one who should apologize is me, for unreasonably snapping at you."

"No, the fault is mine. I apologize. I often pride myself on my straightforward nature, but in this matter, it seems like I keep avoiding, not daring to face your question. Until recently, I realized that the reason might be that... for me, love and marriage are just one and the same."

"What do you mean? You can't move towards marriage because you haven't loved me?" Trường questioned, deliberately twisting her words to elicit the forbidden word - Love.

Understanding the manipulation, Thanh thought, 'Why is that so difficult for me?' She intimately reached out to hold Trường's hand and said, "You should be a lawyer. Very good with your line of questioning!"

Trường, genuinely perplexed, "Well, I truly don't understand."

Avoiding Trường's expectant gaze, Thanh looked into the distance and whispered, as though to herself, "I can't say I love you when I think I can't move towards marriage. What would people say about a woman who only has a lover and no husband?"

"So that's what it is. Whether near or far, the reason is still because of the duty you feel toward your family that prevents you from thinking of marriage. So what about your own future?"

"My future is Thảo," Thanh replied without hesitation.

Trường nodded gently, "I understand. You willingly sacrifice the intermediate generation."

The apparent casual statement from Thanh, albeit unintentional, helped Trường realize the harsh reality. The love Thanh had for him, even as beautiful as embroidered flowers on silk, could not compare to the two words "bổn phận" (duty) engraved on stone tablets and etched into the hearts of Vietnamese women for generations. Trường raised his head, searching for a confidant beyond the Milky Way, yet found himself lost in the feeling of being adrift amid countless stars.

The next morning, the sky was clear with gentle clouds, bathed in the morning sunlight that gleamed brightly on the extensive cement ground, seemingly endless within the vast compound of the distillery. The crowd of refugees began to leave. The sound of gunfire had ceased. A new era began. Whether it was for good or for bad, who could predict where the winds of change would steer the Vietnam ship.

11. A Military Spouse

The ensuing peaceful days quickly passed. The war between the South and North Vietnam smoldered at first, then rapidly intensified across the southern region, resulting in the first landing of American troops in Đà Nẵng in the mid-1960s. Even though it initially occurred in distant places with unfamiliar names, people in the poor neighborhoods of the city could witness its effects through images of daytime funeral processions or the mournful sounds of temple wooden bells echoing through the night. Gradually, the sound of the wooden bell was no longer a simple, captivating melody that could guide the listener to a familiar house in the neighborhood to express sympathy for a surviving member of the household - whether an old mother or a young wife with small children. Now, many temple bells echoed simultaneously from various places, becoming more intense, resonating from the upper to the lower end of town.

Án, Dung's husband, has been granted permission to return home for Tết, the Vietnamese New Year, with his family. The previous year, after completing his training at the Thủ Đức Military Academy, widely recognized as the premier reserved officer training school in South Vietnam, Án received orders to report for duty in Quảng Trị Province within Military Region 1, tasked with guarding the border with Laos.

Án's uncle, Uncle Tư, held the belief that Án was stationed at a distant outpost due to having a brother enlisted in the northern forces. In truth, rumors circulated that the government aimed to prevent potential conflicts on the battlefield by assigning recruits to regions far from their hometowns, particularly if they had siblings serving on opposing sides.

Án's father frequently lamented Án's unfortunate circumstances to relatives. Despite being the family's most academically accomplished child, Án seemed to be consistently beset by misfortune. After successfully passing the French scholarship exams, which promised him the opportunity to study agricultural engineering in France, Án had eagerly prepared for his departure. However, the National Department of Education unexpectedly announced that two France-bound scholarships would be redirected to the United States. The shifting dynamics of Vietnam's political landscape, with the growing dominance of the United States and the waning influence of France, prompted this change, even as the French government at the Élysée Palace sought ways to retain its former colony.

Within Án's family, a significant question arose: should he accept the scholarship to study in the United States? Family members engaged in discussions, with some offering support. Ultimately, Án declined the opportunity to go to the U.S., citing concerns about racial discrimination in American society. This rationale was often mentioned, yet the true underlying reason, possibly influenced by family members with political leanings toward the North, remained unspoken. To avoid potential arguments and discord within the family, it was a topic best left untouched.

In the end Án remained at home and took the entrance exam for the National Teacher's College in Saigon. Upon graduation, he secured a position as a French literature teacher at Thoại Ngọc Hầu High School, situated near the Hoàng Diệu Bridge, connecting the two banks of the River of Long Xuyên - also Dung's maternal hometown.

On her paternal side, Dung was recognized as the granddaughter of a prominent landowner in Cái Bè. However, Dung's grandfather faced elimination by anti-French forces in a land dispute, compelling Dung's father to sell off hundreds of hectares of valuable land. The proceeds were used to move the family to Saigon to escape imminent danger. Struggling with the unfamiliar world of trade, Dung's father encountered losses and mounting debts, culminating in his tragic decision to end his life by jumping into the river under Bình Lợi Bridge. The downfall of Dung's father in the business world mirrored the fate of many affluent families during the transition to post-feudal society. They fell victim to outdated social prejudices that deemed trade a dishonorable profession, adhering to the hierarchical classification of the Four Classes: First Scholar, Second Farmer, Third Worker, and Fourth Trader.

Subsequently, Dung's mother faced the daunting task of raising her three children alone. At the age of fifteen, Dung had to leave school to contribute to household responsibilities, assisting her mother at the family-run food stall that specialized in serving broken rice - a popular breakfast dish also consumed as a quick lunch. A year later, leveraging her proficiency in French, Dung secured a tutoring position to generate additional income for the family. Despite these efforts, life in Saigon became increasingly difficult for them. As the result, Dung's mother made the decision to relocate the family back to the countryside to live with relatives. There, they established a small eatery at the foot of the Hoàng Diệu Bridge in Long Xuyên City.

Professor Án, like any high school instructor respectfully addressed in the country, was a bachelor and a devoted patron of "Miss Dung's" eatery, visiting every afternoon. Upon completing his lunch, he was courteously accompanied by the gracious owner for a brief stroll on the bridge fondly named in their shared memory as "Ô Thước." This bridge evoked the echoes of a legendary love story where a pair of lovers on opposite sides of the Ngâu river were fated by heaven to meet only once a year, traversing a makeshift bridge formed by gathering crows.

Like any heartwarming love story, they had tied the knot and were blessed with a son. By then, Án had returned to Saigon, and they resided with his parents. However, last year marked a significant change when Án was drafted. The family decided to turn Án's welcome party into an extended family reunion. Án's two uncles, aunts, and a few cousins all gathered to greet him.

Relatives encircled the dining table, eager to hear Án's stories from his time away. Among them was Án's fifteen-year-old youngest brother, affectionately nicknamed 'Tiny Út,' who had patiently waited for his turn to inquire:

"Brother, how was it flying on the plane?"

Swiftly, the older sibling scolded Tiny Út, "You ask that? Well, the plane just flies you up into the sky, what else?"

Án felt a pang of nostalgia for his siblings, their innocence reminiscent of his own past. He hugged the youngest sibling and shared, "Yeah, after the plane ascends, looking down, all you see is rooftops, like a bunch of matchboxes laid flat below."

Curious, Tiny Út asked, "Can you see cars and people on the street, Brother?"

"When it's a little higher, you can't see people anymore, but you can still see vehicles, like ants crawling," Án replied.

The inquisitive older sibling chimed in, "Does the plane go up to the clouds, Brother?"

"Of course. It even goes beyond the clouds and flies even higher," Án affirmed.

Tiny Út, still curious, asked, "What about the clouds, how do they look, Brother?"

"From above, you see clusters of clouds like cotton balls," Án began, but before he could finish, his father intervened, scolding the two young sons, "Why are you asking so much? Let your brother eat and talk to your uncles and cousins."

From the kitchen, Dung brought up a large bowl of chicken curry to the party table. She briefly noticed that the men were laughing joyfully, but their merriment suddenly fell silent. However, two words caught Dung's attention, 'Ngủ đò' (Boat sleeping), sparking her curiosity. Though unfamiliar with the term, Dung's instincts told her there was something mysterious afoot.

After most guests departed, Dung approached her husband:

"Earlier, I overheard those men talking about 'Boat sleeping.' What does that mean?"

Án, startled, sobered up from the beer:

"Um... it's a refined pastime on the Perfume River for scholars and literati in the past. At night, they would take a boat to the middle of the river, under the clear moonlight and cool breeze, to compose extempore poetry or listen to classic songs amidst the vast river scenery. Something like that."

Án's explanation initially made sense to Dung, but she couldn't shake the feeling that there was more to the story, given the secrecy surrounding it. She wondered if such pastimes still occurred in the present.

Seizing an opportunity when Án's Uncle Hai, growing impatient, went to the kitchen urging his wife to go home, Dung asked:

"Uncle Hai, what is 'Boat sleeping'?"

Slightly intoxicated, Uncle Hai scolded her:

"Women and kids... why bother asking about that... It's the rendezvous between 'heroes' and 'boat girls' at the Imperial City."

Dung finally understood. In the evening, with only the couple left, the border of the two states was delineated by a bolster pillow placed across the bed: 'You take your part, and I take mine; that's the extent of our relationship.' Late at night, reflecting on her husband's situation amid the thorns of war, Dung dared not think further.

Recalling the past year, every time she encountered a military Jeep driving into the neighborhood, her palms would sweat profusely, and her feet would drag her back home, praying the vehicle wasn't delivering bad news.

"Now my husband, after rare days of leave to visit family, and I'm still grumbling about him all night," Dung thought, feeling guilty. She decided to heed the advice from the verses of the infamous poem, Kiều[1], 'Close her eyes and take a step. Let's see where the whirlwind of fate takes her.'

Thanks to her compassion, heaven favored them, and a year later, another child arrived - this time, a girl, ensuring a balance since the firstborn was a boy. In reality, it was a pity for 'Lieutenant' Án. During that particular leave near his post in the

Citadel city, he dared not betray his wife's expectations. Fearing teasing from cousins and uncles about his reluctance to partake in the romantic pleasures on the Perfume River while he was there, he responded with double talk to save face, even though he yearned for the simplicity of family life.

The next morning, filled with cheerful anticipation, Án eagerly sifted through his backpack, revealing several trays of Huế specialty sesame candy. He delicately placed a portion on the ancestral altar as an offering while reserving some to share the joy with his parents. With a sense of nostalgia, he explored the drawers of the old bureau desk, uncovering two large firecrackers, remnants from his military academy days. Having safeguarded them until then, Án seized the opportunity to set them off by the pond behind the house, unleashing thunderous bangs that reverberated through the heavens and the earth. He celebrated Tết, shared joy with the neighbors, and, last but not least, commemorated personal victory! Pity befell the innocent fish and shrimp below the pond surface, forced to float belly up in the water.

12. The Quartet Reunion

In the blink of an eye, Sáng, Mỹ Lệ's eldest son studying abroad in France, turned 21. Residing in Bảo Lộc, within the Central Highlands region of Vietnam, Mỹ Lệ telephoned Loan to announce her return to Saigon next week for the renewal of the import-export license for her coffee company. In light of this, Loan contacted Thanh, proposing a gathering among the four "sisters" since Loan and Dung were residing with their in-laws, complicating the prospect of hosting a party.

Thanh, the sole single "sister" among them, frequently opened her home for impromptu get-togethers. However, due to the bustling nature of her burgeoning business - having recently purchased a fifth Volkswagen van for conversion into a school bus - and the oversight of her house's garage expansion, Thanh regretfully declined. Two years after retiring from her nursing career, unexpected family circumstances propelled Thanh into a novel adventure: delving into the taxi and student transportation business.

Regarding Mỹ Lệ, she entered into matrimony with Paul after Năm Chảng graciously withdrew his engagement proposal. In the laborers' neighborhood near the notorious Cầu Muối bridge, rumors circulated about 'Brother Năm's' noble gesture - a fond moniker reserved for Năm Chảng, met with great admiration. The impoverished community, often beneficiaries of Năm Chảng's benevolence, believed he willingly stepped aside for Paul upon learning about Mỹ Lệ's suitor. In reality, Năm Chảng, a formidable figure in the underworld, consistently prioritized personal interests and prestige as he ascended to the status of a big brother.

After Paul conveyed his intention to marry Mỹ Lệ, Năm Chảng saw an opportunity to negotiate a lucrative deal with him, securing a substantial business venture. The French colonial authorities often turned a blind eye to underworld activities, allowing gangs to safeguard entertainment venues. This leniency created avenues for the authorities to exploit tax revenue from establishments like casinos, brothels, and various services catering to the affluent's entertainment needs, including nightclubs and bars.

Năm Chảng's condition for permitting Mỹ Lệ's marriage to Paul was that Paul must obtain permission from the French authorities for Năm Chảng to expand his operations beyond the Saigon market area. Năm Chảng coveted control over the renowned Kim Chung casino, second only to the Đại Thế Giới casino in Cholon. Boss Gauthier, recognizing Paul's value in serving the government, acquiesced to Năm Chảng's proposition. In the eyes of the French, employing strong-arm tactics to uphold order in the city, the specific underworld organization mattered little; the authorities always reaped the benefits of all the Machiavellian maneuvering.

Immediately following the clandestine wedding ceremony, meticulously conducted within the renowned Saigon Notre Dame Cathedral, Paul found himself compelled to relocate his entire family to Đà Lạt, situated some 300 kilometers north of Saigon, owing to pressing personal security concerns arising from the exposure of his identity. They settled into a villa atop a pine-covered hill, overlooking a small stream that meandered around large and small rocks along its banks.

Regrettably, the cool climate of the highland region, though cherished by French expatriates and earning Đà Lạt the moniker 'Paris of the East,' proved unsuitable for Aunt Sáu, Mỹ Lệ's mother, exacerbating her arthritis. A mere six months later, Paul orchestrated the family's relocation to Bảo Lộc, a warmer locale that also reduced the distance to Saigon by a third, facilitating the convenience of his frequent covert missions.

Paul's responsibilities extended beyond his role in the notorious "Second Bureau," where he monitored the internal affairs of the armed religious sects of Cao Đài and Hòa Hảo. Simultaneously, he served MI5, the French Intelligence Agency, tasked with gathering information about the activities of allies in Indochina. He reported directly to the headquarters responsible for Indochina affairs, located in Côn Minh, Southern China.

Despite aligning with major powers such as England, the United States, and Russia within the allied bloc, each nation prioritized its own national interests. Post-World War II, France still clung to aspirations of maintaining colonial rule in Vietnam but harbored concerns that the Allies might exploit its setbacks at home to seize control of its colonial territories.

After relocating to Bảo Lộc, Paul acquired a tea farm and a coffee plantation near the Đạ Huoai River, both overseen by Mỹ Lệ. The tea was exclusively distributed within the country, while the coffee found its way to international markets through France. Historically, only the French or individuals with French citizenship could secure import-export licenses. However, with Vietnam's newfound independence, Mỹ Lệ emerged as the pioneering Vietnamese woman in this domain.

Initially, Mỹ Lệ leaned on Paul's guidance to navigate the intricacies of the family business. Tragically, Paul met his demise at the hands of the Đại Thế Giới casino boss, orchestrated in response to a botched negotiation. Subsequently, Mỹ Lệ assumed sole responsibility for the enterprise. Despite the challenges, whenever she journeyed to Saigon to address administrative matters or engage with the bank, Mỹ Lệ unfailingly set aside time to reconnect with old friends.

Regrettably, Thanh couldn't offer her place for the "Quartet of Colette" gathering this time. In response, Loan took the lead in arranging a welcome party for Mỹ Lệ. She had envisioned utilizing her mother-in-law's vacation house in Thủ Đức for this special occasion. Nestled on a gentle hill between two garden plots, the house boasted numerous enticing fruit trees. Whenever Loan visited with her mother-in-law, thoughts of her close friends lingered, silently wishing for their presence: "If only they were here, so I could treat them." Typically, only Uncle Chín, an uncle of her husband, and his family resided there, tasked with overseeing the house and the garden.

The distant location meant that Loan's mother-in-law infrequently visited the vacation house. Yet, when her lady friends craved the sweet, fragrant custard apples in the garden and cleverly persuaded her into organizing a weekend getaway from the city for their beloved Four-color card game, she would eagerly agree to bring them to the retreat.

Loan's mother-in-law could lack anything, but not a Four-color card game every week. Understanding her mother-in-law's weakness, Loan began whispering cleverly to the 'tricksters' that the fruit garden in Thủ Đức was ripe and waiting for them. Loan's scheme bore fruit as expected, providing the sisters with a wonderful place for a festive gathering and her mother-in-law with the Four-color card game she loves dearly.

The family's vacation house nestled atop a gentle hill, embraced by luxuriant greenery, stood proudly next to Biên Hòa Highway.

Across the road, the bright white villas of Thủ Đức University Village provided a picturesque backdrop. Cars gracefully traversed the highway, navigating the dirt road shaded by two rows of mangrove trees. Turning right at the intersection marked by a bushy tamarin tree, they proceeded toward the front gate.

Crafted from ironwood columns with a gleaming dark brown finish, the two-story wooden house bore a distinctive hexagonal-shaped upper floor. Its windows opened in five directions, inviting the refreshing breeze. It was on this floor that Loan's mother-in-law and her companions gathered, seated around a sturdy wooden plank engaged in their favorite card game.

While the ladies enjoyed their time upstairs, Loan eagerly led her friends and two children to the fruit garden behind the house. Ripe red rambutans delighted everyone, but Loan's enthusiasm directed them to a towering mangosteen tree she had been eager to share.

The mangosteens, full and round, hung from the branches, each fruit bursting with sweet juice. A cool breeze carried the sweet and nostalgic scent of fruit blossoms, creating a rare sense of peace and comfort for Mỹ Lệ - a woman seemingly destined to overcome fate. Dreamily looking into the distance, she embraced old memories flooding back - a time when the group gathered for photos by ancient trees in Bờ-rô's shaded garden, sat in a circle on the grass carpet in front of Bách Thảo's botanical garden, next to clusters of golden daisies glowing in the sun.

There were moments captured with abundant longan trees in Long Thành's garden, or the durian and mangosteen orchards in Lái Thiêu, followed by the plum orchard in Mỹ Tho and the star apple fruit orchard in Cai Lậy.

Suddenly, Loan's voice broke through, pulling Mỹ Lệ back to reality,

"Let me check with Auntie Chín, the gardener's wife, to see if she can pack a few mangosteens for the kids to enjoy at home."

Loan turned to Mỹ Lệ, guiding her toward the garden near the Hibiscus hedge fence. There, she proudly pointed out a bushy guava tree adorned with ripe, glossy green fruits, some tinged with a hint of light yellow. Retrieving a small package from her handbag, Loan handed it to Mỹ Lệ, playfully asking, "Does this suit your taste?" Recalling from their childhood that Mỹ Lệ favored spicy food, Loan had prepared a package in her purse that morning to ensure she didn't forget. Mỹ Lệ had a habit of dipping most fruits, whether sour like tamarind and mango, bitter like pomelo, or sweet like plums, in chili salt before indulging.

The sisters gathered around, picking and savoring the guavas, but Loan was eager to guide them back to the rambutan trees. Observing this scene, Dung felt compelled to remind everyone, "Indulge in whatever you desire, but make sure to leave some space for later. I've brought an abundance of cakes, fruit jams, and confectionery." The unanimous decision was made to gather at the picnic table beneath the sprawling jackfruit tree. The diligent gardener had already added two plastic chairs for the two children alongside the four existing stone seats. However, the two youngsters remained entranced by the fruits in the garden and were reluctant to join the group.

Loan, noting the time, suspected that her mother-in-law's card game might conclude soon. She subtly hinted, "It might be time to kick off our celebration." Thanh and Dung hurriedly unpacked the food from the baskets, while Loan called upon the gardener's wife to bring plates and dishes to set up the complete table. Thanh meticulously arranged the powder cakes on a plate. Ordinarily, she would have ordered them from Dung, but this time, with Dung occupied creating confectionery for her customers, Thanh purchased the powder cakes from the daughter of her former home economics teacher.

Mrs. Sửu, the beloved teacher, played a significant role in their school memories, especially her memorable scolding that they still reminisced about: "The four of you are like four demons, not like four virtues as other girls are." Whenever the four friends had the chance to meet her, she would recount the same story of Loan's ambitious attempt to achieve a higher score in her class. The "student" Loan once added ink to dye her pickled cucumber to a perfect green.

Carefully, Dung retrieved a box of 'Choux' cakes from the basket and placed it on the tray alongside the mangosteen jam, all crafted by her own hands. Meanwhile, Mỹ Lệ delved into her bag, producing a package of tea buds and fresh tea leaves that she had arranged for a picker to gather for her the previous day. She handed the bundle to Loan, requesting the garden keeper to brew a pot of tea for the sisters.

Philippe, Mỹ Lệ's 12-year-old second child who had accompanied her on the trip to Saigon, engaged in conversation with Thảo outside the garden. Upon spotting the table brimming with delectables, he eagerly approached Mỹ Lệ, his eyes fixated on the array of cake plates and jam dishes. Observing his longing gaze, Dung halted Philippe, picked up a choux cake, and handed it to him. Curious, Philippe inquired, "Why don't I see mooncakes, aunt?"

Mỹ Lệ interjected to enlighten her son, "That's Aunt Thanh's idea, dear. She aims to promote the use of locally sourced products." Loan chimed in, emphasizing Aunt Thanh's revolutionary concept, "Aunt Thanh envisions a transformation. She wants the Mid-Autumn Festival to radiate more of our homeland's essence, so instead of the traditional mooncakes, Aunt Thanh suggests featuring Aunt Dung's powdered cakes."

Dung appeared contemplative as she spoke, "Poor Aunt Thanh, she initially just wanted to assist me in finding employment. Being the owner of a large business, she would generously gift her employees various cakes and confectionery on every festive occasion. One Mid Autumn Festival, she proposed an innovative idea - instead of purchasing mooncakes, she suggested using my powdered cakes as gifts. Thanks to that opportunity, I managed to earn some extra money for my family.

In a silent expression of gratitude, Dung reflected on Thanh's kindness. With her mother-in-law facing serious illness, the daily expenses for medication had been accumulating. To supplement the family income, Dung had been baking cakes and making fruit jams for sale. During the period when her husband Án was away on military duty, and with no one else at home, Thanh played an active role in supporting Dung's family. She accompanied Dung's mother-in-law to the renowned Grall Hospital, a French-built facility, for examinations multiple times, always offering assistance with medication when needed.

In a gesture of appreciation, when Lieutenant Án was sent to study anti-guerrilla tactics with the British military in Malaysia, he visited Singapore and purchased a new model Philips tape recorder as a gift for Thanh, conveying the family's deep gratitude.

Mỹ Lệ sat observing her "buddies" warmly welcoming her, and a sense of joy reminiscent of her youthful days enveloped her. Unable to resist, she commented on the aging sky,

"Celebrating the Mid-Autumn Festival without the romantic moon is just not the same."

Loan smirked mockingly, interjecting,

"Your son Sáng could have a wife by now. Forget about romantic dreams."

Dung scolded Mỹ Lệ,

"It's all your fault. If only you could stay a few more days, we could wait until evening to properly celebrate the Mid-Autumn Festival."

Loan chuckled, teasing Dung,

"Oh, please. Do you think Mỹ Lệ actually misses the legendary Cuội character on the moon? And it wasn't her beau Sứ?"

Thanh glared at Loan, reprimanding her for unintentionally reopening Mỹ Lệ's old emotional wound. Mỹ Lệ resisted with a forced smile,

"It's okay. That's in the past. Oh, by the way... how's he doing now?"

Loan teased her friend, "If you don't care, why bother asking?"

Since the fateful incident at the gravesite with Paul, Mỹ Lệ distanced herself from Sứ, her first love and someone she deeply thought might be her only love in life. However, while the breakup of a first love might be a cherished memory for a man, for women, it is often a sorrowful experience they try to forget. To forget so they can fulfill their expected duties as wives and mothers.

"He's said to have joined the Paramilitary Corps," Thanh replied. Dung made a point of adding, "And still single, if you're interested." All curious eyes turned toward Mỹ Lệ.

"Just leave me out of it, okay!" Mỹ Lệ retorted with a defiant tone. "You guys think I haven't suffered enough?"

To rescue Mỹ Lệ, Loan quickly changed the subject through Thanh, saying, "Talking about Aunt Thanh, I forgot to ask how things are going with the engineer."

Dung, looking at Thanh, added casually, "You're so lucky. Meeting only 'engineers' and 'doctors' all the time."

Besides thinking of Engineer Trương, Dung wanted to bring up Doctor Phước, who was part of the training program for female nurses and had "planted roses" for Thanh's class for over a year.

It had been a long time since Thanh heard about Doctor Phước. The first image that came to Thanh's mind was on a rainy afternoon. Thanh was cycling to school late. As she entered the classroom, wet from the rain, she was called up to the front to submit her homework. Stepping onto the lectern, Thanh slipped and fell into the arms of Doctor Phước, a young doctor just returned to the country from studying in France. What caught the attention of her female classmates more than anything was that the doctor was still single, fitting the ideal type – 'handsome, smart, and from a wealthy family.' In the following days, there was a lot of gossip and whispers among the female students. Some teased Thanh deliberately, while others envied her, believing that the doctor had concocted a scenario to win Thanh's heart.

Loan suddenly remembered something, staring intently at Thanh with a mischievous gleam in her eyes, "You guys reminded me. How's Doctor Phước doing now?"

Mỹ Lệ shrugged, saying, 'He was pressured by his mother, and has settled down now.' Loan unwrapped a piece of mangosteen candy, putting the treat into her mouth, chewed gracefully, just like in the old days. The sour and sweet taste, familiar from childhood, brought back the sky of memories full of nostalgia for Loan. She declared with determination,

"Since you all brought up Doctor Phước, and I'm in a great mood today, let me share something with you..."

Thanh interjected, "What trouble is this lady trying to stir up now?"

"Oh, don't worry. I won't spill too much. I just want to liven things up a bit."

Mỹ Lệ encouraged, "Spill it. We want to hear Thanh's story for a change."

Loan took a sip of tea, savoring the moment before speaking slowly, "I'll let you in on a secret. The secret of the century."

Thanh snapped, "What are you up to now? Be careful. Let's see who has more secrets."

Loan replied casually, "I've got nothing to be afraid of." Her words, a mix of jest and seriousness, carried the ironic tone of a wife estranged from her husband for several years. Loan squinted mischievously, glancing towards Mỹ Lệ and Dung, and continued, "Did you guys know that the couple had been to Long Hải beach one time?"

"What? Why wouldn't I know that?" Mỹ Lệ looked at Thanh accusingly. "I thought there were no secrets among us."

Dung, usually calm, consoled Mỹ Lệ, "Do you remember where you were at that time? A lot was happening, and even if we spoke, you might not have been in the mood to listen." Mỹ Lệ suddenly realized that during that period, when Thanh was taking nursing courses, she was in Bảo Lộc, just starting her import-export career. Shortly after Paul's tragic death, she had to handle everything inside and outside. Understanding what Dung meant by keeping her in the dark about Thanh's newfound love, Mỹ Lệ turned to Loan and playfully scorned, "So, you're pretty good at keeping secrets from me, aren't you?"

Loan defended herself, saying, "Just teasing you guys a bit, no real secrets here." She deliberately savored another piece of mangosteen jam, which Dung had made slightly sour, knowing her friends liked it that way. Raising her head to the sky, Loan relished the sweet and sour flavor not only from the mangosteen in her mouth but also from the tamarind at the entrance of the alley leading to her old house, the guava in the backyard, the plum sold at the fruit stall at the Trung Lương intersection - a popular gateway to the heart of the Mekong Delta, the pomelo in Biên Hòa, the sapodilla in Lái Thiêu, and even from the fruit orchards in one friend's hometown to another's that they had the chance to visit and disturb, taking photos. Loan immersed herself in the frame of memories, cherishing the sweet and deep sisterly feelings. The images of that day when she and Thanh struggled to choose the right swimsuits for Thanh came back, dancing before her eyes. Loan recounted,

"At that time, Doctor Phước organized a leisure trip to Long Hải for the whole class to go to the beach," Loan explained, pausing before pointing at Thanh and continuing, "Our girl here refused because she didn't have a swimsuit and concocted an excuse that she could not obtain permission from Uncle Tư (her father). Well, that may be true if she did actually ask Uncle Tư. You guys know how strict he is; he'd never let his children wear those 'revealing' outfits."

Loan took her time sipping her tea before continuing, "What I want to say is, why, with the absence of just one student like Thanh from the class, did Professor Phước have to drive all the way to her house to meet Uncle Tư, seeking permission for Thanh? 'Monsieur' even promised to personally pick Thanh up to go on the trip with the whole class and return her to the house at the end of the day, so Uncle Tư could be reassured."

Mỹ Lệ interjected, "Oh, seems intriguing, huh?"

Loan teased, "Listen to this. She had to secretly go to my house to try on my swimsuits. And you guys knew how skinny she was back then, while I... wasn't quite as slender..."

Mỹ Lệ retorted sharply, "Stop it, dear! Whoever said you were overweight before that you'd find the need to protect yourself like that."

"Just reminding you guys that once upon a time, I also had curves, okay."

"Fine, your waist is like a frog's. Satisfied? Now tell us, what did those two do besides going to the beach?"

"Well, think about it. A disciplined girl like Thanh, what could she do? I just wanted to tell you guys about my memory of that day when the two of us chose swimsuits at my house. Picking colors, picking styles. Sitting there watching her try it on, up and down. Then adjusting it here and there to make it even. The first time she tried on the maillot, she seemed so awkward. Honestly, I felt like a mother choosing a wedding dress for her child."

Dung chimed in, "Come on, your eldest daughter at most was only eight at that time."

"You know what I meant. At that time, we were all married, with one or two kids, and my 'sister' here... she was still in her girlish days."

Suddenly remembering something, Loan asked, "Who wants to see Thanh's pictures in a swimsuit? I have those photos hidden at my house until now."

"I forbid you, okay?" Thanh ordered, her tone sounding almost pleading. Mỹ Lệ indulged her, "If she doesn't want us to see the pictures, then let it be. And how's the doctor doing?"

Loan delicately sipped her tea, a tinge of regret coloring her tone. "'Monsieur' persisted, but Thanh steadfastly maintained her refusal. Throughout a year of unrelenting pursuit, he endured constant scolding from his mother, pressing him to marry. My heart aches for Thanh; she turned down a potentially favorable marriage for the sake of her family. He hails from affluence, being a doctor from a wealthy family. Even if she had ten families to care for, he could have easily shouldered the responsibility. Nevertheless, Thanh persistently declined his proposal. No matter how much I implored her, she remained resolute in her decision."

As Thanh gazed out at the garden, her eyes caught sight of Thảo standing amidst the plum trees, meticulously counting the fruits. Admiring Thảo's graceful presence in her white schoolgirl long dress, Thanh couldn't help but be filled with warmth and confidence in her decision to postpone marriage. She comforted herself with the realization that Thảo, unlike many in their generation, had the opportunity to complete high school and was now pursuing her dream of becoming a doctor at medical school.

With a faint smile, Thanh sought to conceal a modest pride brimming with a sense of accomplishment. In her reflections, Thảo's success rested on her own efforts and abilities, yet as a mother, Thanh had exerted every effort within her grasp to aid her daughter in realizing her dreams. Thanh felt a deep sense of satisfaction whenever friends or neighbors in Cây Lý hamlet lauded Thảo. Their praises often alluded to the nurturing influence of the "Aunt," expressed through statements like, "Little Thảo comes from Aunt Thanh's training camp," highlighting Thảo's grace not only in words but also in her interactions with others.

Even during significant family events, Thanh's friends playfully teased her, remarking, "It's also an opportunity for her to deliver a moral lecture." On such occasions, Thanh would instruct the household helpers to deliver food to needy families in the area, finding a lesson for Thảo even in the act of sharing food. She consistently reminded Thảo, saying, "See, you must set aside food for the poor before serving our guests at home, to avoid the appearance of serving leftovers to those in need."

Thanh's heightened concern for instilling ethics in Thảo appeared to have roots in various motivations. Part of this inclination might be traced back to familial influences, particularly from her father. Despite his role as a police officer working for the French during the oppressive colonial regime, he remained somewhat of an exception, retaining a sense of reason that guided his daily actions. Returning home after encountering injustice, he routinely shared these incidents during family dinners, ensuring to impart lessons on "how to treat the underprivileged and the outcasts."

Beyond the familial influence, where ethical lessons were regularly echoed by her father, a more profound societal factor seemed to permeate Thanh's subconscious, leading her to be seemingly obsessed with the responsibility of cultivating ethics in her "daughter." Thanh came of age during a prolonged period of historical turmoil, marked by seemingly endless chaos and suffering. She bore witness to death, brutality, and the pervasive ascent of evil. It raises the question: Did her heightened sense of moral duty stem from an instinct to preserve the lineage, recognizing that a nation couldn't endure without its moral compass?

During this time, Philippe had contentedly immersed himself in the pleasure of savoring Aunt Dung's delectable pastries and sweets, relishing the moments of solitude. Finally, an opportunity arose for him to question all his "Aunties." After polishing off the last two pieces of mango candy, Philippe turned his attention to Aunt Thanh's unconventional idea of celebrating the Mid-Autumn Festival with traditional hometown sweets.

He remarked, "Aunties, Choux pastries are not Vietnamese."

Philippe's unexpected query left the ladies perplexed, but Loan stepped in to defend, saying, "Well, since Aunt Dung made them, they must be Vietnamese, no doubt."

Teacher Dung smiled, attempting to clarify for Philippe and prevent any misunderstandings, "You're correct, but the ingredients and preparation methods may differ somewhat from those used in France or elsewhere, for that matter."

Adding a touch of humor, Loan interjected, "You know, even the names of the pastries have been Vietnamized for a long time. If you don't believe me, just ask your grandmother. She calls them 'Nipple cakes.'"

Loan's eyes sparkled mischievously, concealing a playful smile as she continued, "But everyone agrees that Vietnamese 'Nipple cakes' are much better than the French ones!"

Thanh tugged sharply at Loan's clothing, casting her a reproachful look and questioning why she spoke so freely in front of a child without holding back her words. Recognizing Thanh's commitment to imparting valuable lessons to the children, Dung stepped in.

"Loan, you're on the brink of becoming a grandmother, and you still speak so carefreely," Dung admonished.

Loan resisted, asserting, "You guys lack national pride."

Mỹ Lệ, sensing the need to lighten the mood, clapped her hands and laughed heartily before interjecting to rescue her friend. She revisited old stories and pointed at Loan, declaring, "This woman is no different now. I remember in the last year of Cours Moyen (equivalent to sixth grade), we were all grown up. But one day after gym class, as we were changing clothes in the classroom, she stood on a desk and loudly announced, 'You guys, stay away. Whoever stands nearby, be prepared to endure; I'm shaking off my dirty pants.'"

The four sisters burst into laughter, tears streaming down their faces. These tears held the essence of deep emotions, sparkling in the moments of shared joy that would forever reside in their hearts.

Mỹ Lệ's recounted story unintentionally transported Loan back to the carefree days of a girl growing up in luxury, like a rare flower accustomed to receiving admiring glances from friends and family. Little did anyone know that even such a flower couldn't escape the fate of Vietnamese women, drifting along with the nation's fortunes through infrequent peaceful days with calm waves and gentle winds, while facing more frequent tumultuous storms and strong winds. The smile always bloomed on her lips, and elegance radiated outward, but it was a reflexive shield originating from an inexhaustible inner strength to control the pain within, rather than a superficial gesture born to attract life's applause.

This was Loan's state of mind. Though nominally still Nhân's wife, she had been living in the shadows for the past four years. From morning till night, she cared for her mother-in-law and looked after the children.

Nhân, Loan's husband, returned to Vietnam disappointed after graduating from France, as his ideals for serving his homeland did not materialize as expected. According to his father, he was born at the wrong time. Returning to the country after studying in France at a time when the influence of the United States was prevalent, Nhân served in the education sector and witnessed a sea change in the academic approach. Previously, the system leaned towards training intellectual elites with a theoretical emphasis on lofty philosophies, differing from the American tendency to train practical human resources to meet economic and societal development needs. Additionally, internal conflicts, disputes, and infighting emerged. As an outsider, Nhân found it challenging to adapt.

Nhân felt lost in his own homeland and decided to return to France. His plan was to stabilize his life overseas and then bring his family over. However, after two years of work and cohabitation with a French woman, his plans changed. Both Loan and her mother-in-law were disappointed, and the dream of a family reunion seemed to fade away. Nhân's letters became less frequent, and apart from the occasional packages sent to the family, the connection grew thin.

As time passed without a husband, "the market remained busy," to borrow a popular saying. The daughter-in-law sought solace in daily tasks, caring for and educating the children, and attending to her mother-in-law. Luckily, in this case, the daughter-in-law didn't have to struggle to make ends meet like many other women, as her husband's family was relatively well-off for generations. The house was not lacking in servants and helpers. Loan's duty to her mother-in-law was simply to ensure that her betel tray was always filled with betel leaves from Bà Điểm and Hóc Môn, not too young and not too old, just as her mother-in-law preferred. Occasionally, when a hand was needed for her mother-in-law's Four-colour card game, she could always count on Loan. And so, the ship sailed, days turned into months, and the mother-in-law and daughter-in-law harmoniously coexisted.

Suddenly, three semi-naked Japanese men appeared out of nowhere, squatting by the well behind the house. The unexpected sight caught all the guests off guard, except for Loan. She recognized them as Japanese engineers who had come to Vietnam to supervise the renovation of the bridge on the Biên Hòa Highway, which had been in operation for several years. They had rented the three ground-floor rooms at Loan's mother-in-law's vacation home for their stay during their mission in Vietnam. Each evening upon returning home, their first task was to draw water from the well for bathing.

Their presence served as a reminder to Loan that it was time for her party to head back to Saigon before nightfall. She quickly asked her friends to clear the dining table, preparing for the return trip.

Rumors circulated that the Americans built the Biên Hòa Highway for their military planes to land in emergencies when Tân Sơn Nhất Airport was under attack. However, those in the know believed it was part of a long-term infrastructure development plan. Nevertheless, the Japanese government, as part of the Second World War's reparations program, had completed a portion of this project.

On the journey back, as the car turned left onto the highway, Dung shifted her gaze towards Long Thành, overwhelmed by a pang of longing for her husband. It had been just a little over two years since the tragic incident. Following his military service, Án, her husband, had sought employment as a trainer at the Rural Construction Training Center in Vũng Tàu. However, fate took an unfortunate turn when, on his way home one day, the bus he was on struck a landmine and erupted in an explosion.

Dung personally went to the Long Thành intersection to retrieve her husband's remains, cherishing memories of her kind and exemplary partner. Án had been devoted to his wife, attentive to his children, and showed utmost respect to his parents. The loss left a void that lingered, and Dung couldn't help but reflect on the warmth and love that defined her late husband's character.

She made a solemn commitment to herself, vowing to care for her mother-in-law in Án's stead. Several years prior, Án had reclaimed the tape recorder he had once gifted to Thanh. However, this wasn't for recording the latest Vietnamese or French music as per the prevailing trend. Due to the government's implementation of the Law on the Protection of Morality, which banned activities such as gambling, prostitution, and dancing, many individuals discreetly organized home parties. Faced with such restrictions, people had to substitute live bands with tape recorders.

Meanwhile, Án utilized the recording device to capture the voices and messages of his parents. His commitment went further, extending to Rạch Kiến, where he visited various relatives' households, recording the words of his grandparents, aunts, uncles, and great aunts. He sought to preserve the cherished voices that had shaped his identity. Unfortunately, Án departed suddenly, leaving behind no farewell for his wife and children. War, with its cruel dynamics, could transform a pure soul into a killer or erase its existence in the blink of an eye.

As Thanh approached her home at the far end of town, approximately two kilometers away, the road became increasingly congested. Vehicles were lined up along the historic An Thông Hạ canal, patiently awaiting their turn to cross the U-shaped bridge. In the distance, two American military bulldozers maneuvered on the opposite side of the waterway - one advancing, the other retreating - raising and lowering their massive buckets in front of each vehicle. A cloud of dust enveloped the scene as they demolished two rice warehouses that had stood abandoned for several years on the canal's bank.

In the place of the demolished warehouses, rumors circulated that the Americans planned to construct a military supply depot and a military compound. Each afternoon, after a day of seemingly moving mountains, young American soldiers, neatly dressed in civilian clothes - jeans and short-sleeved shirts of various colors - wandered through the streets. Some confidently engaged with the locals, expressing a zest for life and seeking conversations with hospitable families. They were particularly interested in households whose children knew some English, eager to learn more about Vietnamese culture.

Meanwhile, other young conscripts were drawn to the lively sounds of music emanating from bars and pubs, scattered both nearby and in the distance.

In the midst of the turbulent battlefields, the rear of Saigon reverberated with music, drowning out the dissonance of gunfire and bombs. As night fell, the haunting sound of bamboo tocsin from someone's funerals urged wandering souls to find their resting peace, while in the daylight, the music enticed people into a realm of gambling, where the stakes were nothing less than the fate of a lifetime or even one's own life.

The romantic melodies, emerging after the 1954 migration from the North to the South, initially portrayed the war through a rosy lens - gentle and ethereal, akin to steps on clouds no longer fitting. Over time, however, the music took on a more grounded, worldly tone. Lyrics spoke of harsh realities like "Those who died twice, their flesh shattered," or "He comes back, perhaps in a wooden box adorned with flowers; he comes back on a stretcher... he comes back, a crippled general with an amputated leg."[2] In impoverished neighborhoods, people sought solace in forgetfulness through these melancholic tunes. Radios had become a common possession, broadcasting melodies throughout the day, resonating from the beginning to the end of the alley. Even children had memorized the poignant verses:

"Tomorrow is someone else's wedding,

Why is the mountain girl Phà Ca still sad."[3]

The emotions conveyed ranged from the sorrow of a mountain girl to the despair of a sedge mat seller:

"This mat I won't sell, if I can't find you...

Oh... if I can't find you, I will use it to lay my head on every night.

...The Cà Mau mat boat has anchored on the banks of Ngã Bảy,

why doesn't the girl from the past come out to greet."[4]

The voices of singers Thanh Nga, Út Bạch Lan, and Út Trà Ôn sometimes soared to touch the heavens, and at other times descended low to the thick earth.

Outside, on the street, immersed in the sparkling lights illuminating the universe, the resounding voice of Thái Thanh filled the air, echoing the soul of rivers and mountains, resonating with joyous melodies following each step of the pioneer's marching procession on the main road to the South - Con Đường Cái Quan[5]. The singing brought to life the steps of exploration, expanding horizons, and arousing belief through the radiance of a bygone era.

If that was the call of the sunflower silently reproaching the endless night, then in the corner of the dance floor, the heartbeat was the voice of a wandering rose in the mist, embracing dreams of dawn that existed only in memories. The enchanting voice of Thanh Thúy filled countless glasses with wine, toasting to pilots after night flights[6], soldiers just separated from fallen comrades on the battlefield, or lonely individuals trying to forget in the haze of alcohol and cigarette smoke. It was a delicate voice that encapsulated the entire essence of Vietnamese women - steeped in hidden sorrows, yet enduring without complaints through generations.

- The End -

Notes

1. Poem: 'Đoạn Trường Tân Thanh' (The Tale of Kiều); Author: Nguyễn Du.
2. Song: 'Kỷ Vật Cho Em'; Songwriter: Phạm Duy.
3. Play: 'Người Vợ Không Bao Giờ Cưới'; Playwright: Kiên Giang.
4. Play: 'Tình Anh Bán Chiếu'; Playwright: Viễn Châu.
5. Song: 'Trường Ca Con Đường Cái Quan'; Songwriter: Phạm Duy.
6. Song: 'Một Chuyến Bay Đêm'; Songwriters: Song Ngọc & Hoài Linh.

Author

Vinh Quyen Tang
(Tăng Quyền Vinh)
Ottawa, Canada.

Books published:

1. Bên Kia Bến Đỗ, 2021
2. Đứa Con An Giang, 2022
3. Lu nước ngọt, 2023
4. Nails Tình Thương, 2023
5. The Boy From An Giang: A Journey Through AI-Assisted Translation, 2023 (Under revision)
6. The Precious Quartet (Selected Tales from Bên Kia Bến Đỗ), 2024

ISBN 978-1-7381921-2-0

www.ingramcontent.com/pod-product-compliance
Lightning Source LLC
Chambersburg PA
CBHW030903200726
48289CB00003B/882